SBN-10:0-9987309-4-7
ISBN-13:978-0-9987309-4-3

Sparks in Spearfish

© 2017 Kari Trumbo

Published by Kari Trumbo, All Rights Reserved

All rights reserved. No part of this publication may be reproduced, stored in a retrieval system, or transmitted in any form by any means, without the prior written consent of the author. Thank you for respecting the author's work.

Scripture quotations are from the King James Version of the Bible

Author's note: This is a work of fiction. All locations, characters, names, and actions are a product of the author's overactive imagination. Any resemblance, however subtle, to living persons or actual places and events are coincidental.

Sparks in Spearfish

Seven Brides of South Dakota: Book 5

KARI TRUMBO

Spearfish Normal School
Spearfish, South Dakota, 1895

Chapter One

"I'll hate you 'til the day you die, Barton Oleson!" Lula Arnsby ran her hand through her hair, which was clumping under the weight of the butter the wretched Barton just mashed into it. In the South Dakota heat, even in spring, it would curdle in no time.

He stopped running and turned back to her. "Better run home and wash up, butter cup, before you attract flies!" He dashed around to the front of the large brick boarding school.

Lula blinked back the tears she'd held in all year. Barton had tormented her since the very first day she'd joined his class at the Spearfish Normal School. Though Mrs. Tomlinson was strict, she'd never managed to catch Barton in the act, leaving Lula to look like a spoiled child, complaining about him with no cause. At just sixteen, and having been schooled close to home her whole life, she'd been unprepared for boarding school. She'd even begun to question if she wanted to stay. It was now the final term of the year and she would go home, back to Deadwood, to see her family. Her brother-in-law Beau would have wise words. She'd wanted to be the very first Arnsby to have a certificate, to hold an important job. But the longer she stayed, the less she wanted it. Teaching was a noble profession, something she could aspire to, but not if she couldn't even convince one boy to leave her be.

At least she only had one more year with him, then she'd never see his face again. He'd never choose to be a teacher, so his time would be done at the end of primary school. He came from a long line of cowboys, or so he liked to boast. Teaching would never interest him. She could be free then, but she'd have to stay through one more year of torment. Did she have the will?

Her most dear friend, Izzy, ran up to her. Izzy's dark braids bouncing against her back as she ran. "Lula, what in tarnation happened to you?" She fingered one of the clumped curls and grimaced. "That's horrible. I can't believe anyone would do that to you after the announcement this morning."

Lula's heart tripped. "What announcement?" She hadn't been there for the morning reading. *Someone* had put tobacco juice on her seat and it had soaked through her best beige skirt. It was, even now, soaking in a wash tub to get the stain out.

"We're to conserve water. No bathing, only the washbasin until it rains. The water in the well is too low."

"But...surely they would consider this necessary!" She couldn't keep the shriek from her voice. Even now, her hair was thick and the flies swarmed above her head.

"We'd better go talk to Mrs. Keets." Izzy wrapped a chubby

protective arm around her waist, but avoided touching her hair.

Mrs. Keets was the dorm matron, and probably a teacher of some other class, but Lula had never paid much attention. After-class hours were full of preparing for the next day, reading, and cleaning up whatever mess Barton had left for her.

"That boy is a menace." Izzy clicked her tongue, her blue eyes sparking indignant anger. "You'd think he'd tire of picking on you."

"I wouldn't think. He hasn't missed a single day for an entire term. I'll be so glad to go home and be rid of him for a while." The tears welled up, yet again. He was making a failure out of her. Admitting to Beau and Ruby that she couldn't do another year would be so disappointing. They'd sacrificed so much to send her.

Izzy ushered her into the small apartment where Mrs. Keets lived, at least for the school year. The matronly woman smiled for a moment, then her nose twitched.

"Miss Arnsby. What sort of nonsense have you gotten yourself into now?" She stepped forward and yanked a clump of Lula's hair closer to her face. "What is this?"

Lula couldn't hold back the waver in her voice. "It's Barton again. He's put butter in my hair!"

"And just how is a boy supposed to get a hold of butter? They aren't allowed in the kitchens. I find that I am finished listening to you dither on about Barton. He's been nothing but an exceptional student since the very first day he came. However, *you've* done nothing but complain about him since the day you arrived. Until you can temper your urges to get Barton Oleson in trouble, you are not allowed to wash your hair. It will remain that way until you decide to meet with him and apologize for your troublesome behavior. I think I'll find that by tomorrow, you'll relent and I won't hear any more about Barton." The wide-shouldered teacher turned from her and crossed her arms, no doubt waiting for her to beg to apologize that instant. She couldn't do that, though washing was so tempting.

Lula stood for a moment considering what she could say, then her anger built. "Do you think I put this in my hair myself?"

Mrs. Keets waved her hand, not bothering to turn back to face her. "It isn't of any consequence. You've said that you want to teach, Miss Arnsby. Part of teaching is figuring out how to manage students bigger, stronger, and sometimes, when you first get out of school, older than you. If Barton is bothering you...learn to manage him, or find a new profession."

Izzy drew her out of the room before she said more that she would regret. "I might be able to help you get most of it out," she whispered.

"If you do that, it will only get us both in trouble. How I hate that boy. How will I ever apologize to him?"

Izzy shook her head and bit her lip. "I'm not sure, but I'm afraid I would've asked to do it right away. How are you going to sleep tonight with that?"

Lula fingered her hair once more. "If it wasn't so completely horrible, I'd just leave it. I don't owe him anything. He owes *me* an apology, not the other way around."

"That's never going to happen, you and I both know it. Barton is from Belle Fourche, cattle money. His pa probably pays near a fortune to make sure he stays out of trouble."

"I'm not so lucky." Lula opened the hall door to the dorm she shared with fifteen other girls, then waited. "I may as well just get this over with.

I have to get it out before class tomorrow, and I can't sleep like this."

"Godspeed," Izzy whispered and closed the door before the other girls could notice.

Lula hid in the shadows as she made her way back to Mrs. Keets's room. She knocked on the apartment door and Mrs. Keets answered. Inside, Barton and a male teacher waited. Mrs. Keets frowned. "Come to your senses so quickly? Perhaps there's hope for you, yet."

Lula stepped into the room and Barton's blue eyes caught and held hers, if he wasn't such a bully, those eyes would've had her heart. She resisted the urge to scowl and back away. His warm brown hair was always perfect, even after wearing a hat, and his clothes never had a spot. He was handsome and knew it, right down to the fancy leather of his boots.

"Lula." He raised an insufferable eyebrow. If things had been different between them, she might like that particular quirk. It reminded her, subtly, of Beau.

She drew rein on her thoughts as she took in a shallow breath. She had no idea what Beau would do in her situation, but mousing around, dreaming of home probably wasn't it. "I'm sorry for trying to get you in trouble, Barton," she whispered, chin down.

He stepped forward, so close the scent of leather lingered over her, but she couldn't back away or she'd look rude, combative. Even if that's exactly how she felt, Mrs. Keets couldn't know that. This had to go perfectly so she could clean up, even her white shirtwaist would need to be washed now.

"And are you sorry for those hateful words you spoke in the courtyard?" he whispered. He angled his head down to look her right in the eyes. Blast! Why did he have to have such pretty eyes?

She narrowed her own at him. He could make her say them, but she'd never feel any differently. "Yes."

"Say it." He prodded, his voice a caress from a foot away.

She sighed and closed her eyes to block the view of a face too handsome to hate, but she did, just the same. "I'm sorry I said that I hate you."

He laughed. "See, that wasn't so hard. It was almost like we had a real...conversation." He managed to break through her resolve to avert her eyes, then, seeing the intensity of his gaze, she had to look away.

She held her breath and bit her tongue, too afraid Mrs. Keets would take back her promise.

The matron touched her on the shoulder. "That's fine. Let's go to the kitchen and get you cleaned up. It's looking like it will be a grand day tomorrow."

If only it were the last day. She fisted her skirt to keep from screaming at the smug cowboy, staring at her as she turned to leave.

Spearfish Normal School, 1897

Chapter Two

Lula smiled at her reflection in the mirror above her dresser. She'd stayed with the school for two long years, biting her tongue at every turn just to make it here, her first day of teacher training. A year from now, she'd have her certificate and could apply for a position at some small South Dakota school. She untied the bow at her collar and tried again. It would have to be perfect. She wanted to impress the teacher and the other students. And it had been so long since she'd dressed to look nice, instead of to hide from Barton.

Faithful Izzy stood behind her and rested her hands on Lula's shoulders. "You look just perfect. We should get to class a little early so we can find good seats and watch who comes in. I wonder if we'll know anyone else?"

"None of the other students had interest in teaching, but anything is possible." As long as one particular boy stayed far away, the whole state of South Dakota could join the class and she'd still be happy.

Izzy gathered her paper, pencils, and book and waited for Lula. The mirror caught Lula one last time and she couldn't help being pleased. She hadn't worn her curls down at school since Barton had buttered them. The smile slipped from her face. Thinking of him for another moment would ruin a perfectly good start to a new year, and she wouldn't sacrifice another. He'd made her last two years of school torment, but this, this year she would enjoy.

She grabbed her own supplies and followed Izzy to a part of the school she'd never been in before. It was within the large brick three-story administration building. The room smelled of the solution used to clean the blackboard, but if this was like the rest of the school, in a few days, only the smell of chalk would linger. A few rows of desks large enough for adults ran the length of the yellow room, with grand high ceilings and windows that spread almost from her knee to well above her head, letting the bright sun in. Izzy chose a desk in the very middle of the room. Lula followed, sitting next to her so they could talk before class. They were the first to enter and the silence in the room kept them from speaking beyond muffled whispers. The tin ceiling was white with fresh paint, the floors a gleaming oiled wood. She'd heard that the professor who ran the school taught the classes for teachers. He'd been there for many years. As the clock ticked the minutes, excitement built in her stomach.

Six other women and eight men Lula didn't recognize slowly found seats within the room. Their muffled noises bounced off the walls, creating enough racket that she and Izzy couldn't talk. Down the hall, the sound of children excited by their first day made its way into the room, and Lula's heart exalted with them.

She couldn't wait to experience that joy of bringing young people together to learn! Her own little country school had been wonderful, filled with friends and learning. But when she'd decided, at age fifteen, that she wanted to teach, Beau and Ruby had arranged for her to come to Spearfish the following year, to get the best schooling they could afford, before she started training for her certificate. Now, one year away from her goal, and she was finally back to a place where she could enjoy herself and focus on learning.

Izzy gasped to her right and her eyes grew wide as she stared at a spot over Lula's right shoulder. Lula spun in her seat to see what had disturbed her, just as one of her precious curls was tugged. A sick feeling landed in her stomach. She didn't need much help interpreting the look of horror on Izzy's face. She knew.

Lula slowly turned all the way to face the boy who'd tormented her for two long years. Instead of the normal brown trousers and crisp white shirt of a student, he wore a suit with a neat string tie. His collar was high, covering most of his neck, but his blue eye sparkled with contained mischief. Barton had grown up over the summer and now he was more handsome than ever.

"If it isn't Miss Arnsby? Good to see a familiar face." His lip curved up in a playful smile that made his face too irresistible by far. For years, Barton had teased her about wanting to be a schoolmarm, and now, of all the places he could be, what could he possibly be doing in her class?

Barton strode toward his new classroom and said a quick prayer that Lula hadn't changed her mind or switched schools on him, not that teaching schools were abundant anywhere and none were closer than Spearfish Normal for the people of the Hills. He paused outside the door to calm his nerves. At the end of term last year, after two years of trying to get Lula's attention, he'd almost given up. Almost. That girl was a part of him as much as his arm, and though he could survive without either, he'd prefer not.

The last day of school, primary graduation, his pa had arrived to collect him and his things to go home. Lula's parents arrived also, and he watched their tearful reunion, but there was something about Lula's tears that were *off*. And the way her pa had strode off, angry-like, told him he might be in a heap of trouble. His pa had come around to find him a while later and he'd known he would get a talk, maybe more. His pa was silent mad, and that was the scariest kind. That ride back to Belle Fourche gave him plenty of time to think about how to get Pa out of his anger, but nothing worked.

When they'd gotten home, Pa had unhitched the wagon and told him to wait in the wood shed. It had been the longest yet shortest wait of his life. After his pa had given him a whippen', he'd set him on a stump out back of the wood shed, man to future man, and explained to him there were ways to treat a young lady, and how he'd been acting wasn't it. He could remember now how his hands had trembled as he'd told his pa how pretty she was with her mass of blonde curls. How it had all started so innocently. He'd just wanted to touch one curl...but she'd yanked her head away and accused him of pulling. He hadn't, he'd just been holding, touching the softness.

Sparks in Spearfish

Every time she'd turn red and get angry with him, it gave him more fuel. Those blue eyes... Even when she said she hated him, she was talking to him, and that was all that mattered.

After he'd *pulled* her hair, she'd branded him trouble and he'd done his best to oblige. If that would be the only attention she'd give him, he'd take it. He'd tested every limit to make sure she thought about him every single day, but had to make sure he was never caught, or his pa wouldn't let him come back. His three older brothers had the ranch well in hand. They'd all barely made it through school, since it had seemed a waste of time to them. He was pretty sure his oldest brother, Conrad, couldn't read. Barton had been interested in learning, but if he couldn't behave in school, he'd have to join his brothers back at the ranch.

Barton had asked his pa that day, behind the wood shed, if he could go back to school and do the teacher training over the summer so he could be finished by the time school started and apply for the one assistant position they offered. It was his only chance to see Lula again and to either convince her to think about him every day in a wholly other fashion...or let her go.

Now that he was here, he took a deep breath and swung into the room, stopped short by the shock of blonde curls, the only thing his vision would allow. She'd even worn her hair down for the occasion, she hadn't since he'd buttered those locks over a year ago. He had to fight every impulse not to bury his face in them. He'd never felt anything softer. As he walked by, her friend Izzy saw him. He heard the gasp and saw her look of utter shock. His muscles moved as if he couldn't control them and he reached out, tugging on one of those locks of glorious golden curl.

She spun around and faced him, blue fire in her eyes.

My, my girl is spunky. She stood and shoved her hands on her hips.

"Barton Oleson, I don't know what you're doing here, but you will *not* ruin this for me. I've waited two long years to be free of you and I won't be bullied during my final year."

He let the smile he'd been told looked thoroughly wicked frame his face. "That's *Mr.* Oleson. I've been given the professor's assistant job this term."

All the color drained from her face. He hadn't meant for it to come across as a threat. Only one step distanced him from her and he closed the gap to catch her if her knees went faint, a real possibility by the look of her.

"No. How could you...?"

He let his voice drop to a whisper and reveled in the intimate feeling it gave. "I was here all summer, training for this job." He tightened his jaw and rested his hand on her shoulder to direct her to sit before she collapsed. Her shoulder was strong, the fabric of her shirt soft. And she wasn't running from him, because she couldn't. She flung a piercing glare at him and shrugged off his hand.

He smiled, taking his wandering thoughts under control. "Just so we're clear, Miss Arnsby. *I'm* what stands between you and your teaching certificate."

She dropped into her seat, batting away the tears he could see forming. Had he really tormented her so badly that she would cry? Had his words scared her so? His father's condemnation came back to haunt him and he regretted his statement immediately. He leaned over her desk so no one else might hear.

"Miss Arnsby, I don't think you'll have any issue with the class. You've borne much more difficult trials." Then he stood and went to the front desk where he'd been told to arrange the professor's notes. He wouldn't actually be teaching until the second half of the year. Which was good. If he'd had to stand up in front of Lula and her cohorts with his hands itching to take her out in the hall, explain what his pa had told him, and bury his hands in her hair and his face in her neck, he'd make a fool of himself. Something he prided himself on never doing.

Professor Cook strode into the room and walked to the front. Barton had gotten to know him well over the last three months. He was a hard man, but a fair one. Professor Cook nodded at him. "Stick to the front so that you're ready if I need anything." He didn't bother to whisper.

Barton had always preferred the back of the classroom with the rest of the boys, but he wouldn't encourage misbehavior by flouting what the professor said, though he'd rather sit nearer to Lula. Though everyone in the room was almost an adult, either seventeen or eighteen, the temptation would still be there. He took a seat two ahead of Lula, catching her eye once again as he approached. Her eyes still gleamed with unshed tears. As he sat, he could feel the heat of her glare boring into his back. He had a mountain of a mess to clean up and only nine months to do it.

Chapter Three

Lula stumbled back to her room after the noon dismissal, rushing to avoid any more talk with Barton. He'd wanted to, she could read it on his face as the noon time approached. He'd turned and tried to catch her eye, but she'd persevered and ignored him. When the clock struck noon, she'd gathered her things, left Izzy behind, and ran. It might not be ladylike, but she couldn't bear another year of tears hidden in the broom closet. She'd gotten to know the cleaning staff quiet well the last few years, but they didn't want to see her any more than she wanted to see them.

How could life be so cruel? Beau and Ruby had to save to send her to such a nice school, and she'd been so excited. With Barton, every hope of a good year died like cut flowers. She slumped on the bed and stared at her trunk. Should she give up and just fill it. Go home? All this time, she'd counted on this year. This one year. It would be the best experience, the one she looked back on with joy in her older years. What if he made sure she didn't graduate? Hadn't he threatened just that? *Miss Arnsby, I'm what's standing between you and your certificate...* If it weren't a threat, it certainly was a challenge. She yanked the coverlet over her head. It was too much to think about. Her stomach grumbled against her stays. She'd avoided breakfast that morning because of nerves, but now she was starving and she wouldn't go to the cafeteria for lunch. She couldn't avoid it forever, but he was sure to be there. Unless *teachers* ate somewhere else. He was her teacher. Had been at school all summer to get ahead of her, to lord his position over her.

Beau and Ruby were so proud of her. How could she let them down by asking to come home on the very first day? It wasn't an easy trip from Deadwood to Spearfish, and not something she could ask of them lightly. Even so, it could be days before they were able to arrange a way to get her home. She had to stay, there was no choice. She stood from her bed and kicked her trunk. Why did Barton always have to ruin everything?

She strode to and sat before her mirror, pulling out all of her hairpins that had swept her hair out of her face, but showed off her curls. They had to be put away. She'd found out after Barton had buttered her hair that he carried a pocket knife with him wherever he went, and she'd had visions of him hacking off her hair. From that day on, she'd worn it in a bun or roll but always up and out of his reach. He'd looked so sullen the first day she'd worn it up. She'd considered herself a victor that one time, ruining whatever he'd planned.

Finishing with her hair, she pressed her pretty moleskin gray walking skirt, her hands fluttering slightly over the soft fabric. She'd taken to wearing black skirts after Barton had stained her light one's with everything from tobacco to food. This one would be an easy target. But he was a teacher now...surely he wouldn't pull anything so childish...

She yanked open her dresser drawer and pulled out the one black walking skirt she'd brought. She'd learned early on in her life at Spearfish Normal, better to be safe than sorry. Walking around with a deep brown stain on her rear from tobacco juice taught her that. It was really too bad, she'd been rather free-willed before Barton. Her sister's Ruby and Frances had both warned her she'd need to abandon that though, and they were right. Teaching young boys like Barton required strict behavior, not frivolous whimsy.

Her lunch period was drawing to a close and she couldn't be late back to class, she had to change quickly. Her stomach protested her forgetfulness and she patted her belly absentmindedly. She'd eat later, after she'd prepared to deal with Barton for the rest of the day.

She fixed her tie one last time and frowned. The frightened little girl from the last two years stared back at her. How had she let him control every part of her life? From her hair to her clothes, it was all to keep him from getting to her and he still had, in every way. Even now, she was hungry because she'd needed to fix herself. He'd controlled her without even trying. She stomped her foot. The school could give her rules and she'd follow them, but she wouldn't change again for Barton Oleson, and if he tried anything, she'd take what she learned at teacher training and correct him ... or die of embarrassment.

She hadn't been at lunch. He'd walked the cafeteria after hastily devouring his own meal. Then, he'd made it appear he was proctoring the noon, but it was all show. He'd wanted to see her. Food wasn't allowed in the dorm rooms and she hadn't come to eat, so where could she be? Worry spiked through him as the clock clicked ever closer to one. He'd have to run up to class shortly and get Professor Cook's notes ready and the board wiped clean. Had she been so worried about seeing him that she would skip lunch? How many meals would she miss just to avoid him?

He searched the hallway on his way to class, but Buttercup wasn't lurking anywhere. The campus wasn't large enough for her to evade him forever. He pushed the door open to find her sitting calmly in her seat, her hair completely swept up in a delicate roll that hid all but its color. She'd changed from the pretty skirt she'd worn earlier to a black one that looked more like widow's weeds than a choice a young woman would intentionally make. Had she changed because of him? The empty room made him bold. He had to know.

He sat in the desk in front of her and turned to face her. She pushed herself as far back in the desk as possible to get away from him. How had he never noticed what his actions had done? How had he been so oblivious that he could think any attention, even if it embarrassed or hurt her, was enough? Because it meant he was on her mind. He'd go back and change every moment of it if she wouldn't fear him.

"I know you aren't happy that I'm here." He kept his voice low and his head down. "You probably still hate me and I deserve that. But I worked really hard to be here." He searched for her eyes, blue pools of heat and light. "I want to start over, if it's possible. I'm sorry for the things I did to you. I was a stupid boy. Can we at least try to get along for this term?"

She bit her lip and he clenched his fist in his lap to keep from running his thumb over it to stop her. He didn't even want her to hurt that little bit, and especially not on his account.

"Mr. Oleson, I will give you the respect you're due as my teacher, and I forgive you because I must as a woman of God, but I have no desire to start over with you, ever." Her voice wavered and he saw the tears forming behind her eyes in glistening tiny droplets at the rim. He pulled out his handkerchief and handed it to her.

"Believe it or not. I never, ever wanted to make you cry." He stood and she tried to give him back his handkerchief without putting it to use. "Keep it." He turned away from her and strode to the desk to arrange the notes for the afternoon class and to ready the board. How did she get to him? She'd had his heart from the very first moment he'd laid eyes on her, but she would need to be coaxed. He had all year to convince her of his intentions, and they *were* honorable, at least, they were now. Teaching had never been one of his passions, he still loved breaking horses and chasing down beeves, but if he had to earn a teaching certificate in order to convince the woman he couldn't live without that he was worthwhile, so be it. He'd work his fingers to the bone if he had to.

He'd put in grueling hours all summer long to complete an entire year of training in three months. The first man to ever do it, and the professor was proud of his accomplishment. Having the professor on his side would help. If anyone found out he was attempting to court a student, he could find himself sent home, his internship incomplete. It was a risk he was willing to take for Lula.

Keeping his head angled down, he watched her. She folded and tucked away his handkerchief. Would she keep it close by? Would she think about his words? How could he turn back all the rotten things he'd done and why hadn't he asked his pa that question after the first year of school? He could've done better the second. He'd tormented her. But even now, the thought of engaging her in another battle of wills thrilled his blood. She was fun to fight with, always ready for him. Too ready. He wanted to pull out every pin holding her hair out of reach and throw it away, because it was his fault.

Professor Cook entered the room. "Thank you, Mr. Oleson. You may take your seat while we wait for the other students."

There were two seats available in front of Lula, the one he'd sat in that morning, and the one he'd been sitting in just a few minutes before. He slid to a stop before of the front seat, but the draw to be near her was too great. He took the extra few steps and sat in front of her. She'd have to get used to being near him, whether she liked it or not.

Chapter Four

How could she pay one whit of attention with him sitting right there? Just in front of her. If their positions had been switched, he'd have flicked her ears. Of all the places he could've chosen, why did he have to sit right in front of her? And just what did he mean by apologizing out of nowhere. He'd never had to apologize for anything in his life. The last few years he'd gotten off free, while she'd paid the price of being the one to complain. No one liked a squeaky wheel.

She pried her gaze from the back of his head and focused on the professor, a middling man with a narrow face and giant mustache that ate his upper lip. His collar was so high it seemed to notch his head at a painful angle, but obviously didn't hinder his speech. He rattled on as if he could do the course while asleep.

His voice droned to her ears, like a wagon wheel crunching over gravel on a long ride. "Students. I would like an essay about the new theories evolving in education. The idea that children should do more than recite, but engage. Do you think these new theories have a future, why or why not? I want it on my desk by Thursday morning. Dismissed."

Barton appeared at her desk before she could even close her notebook. "Can I walk you back to your dorm, or perhaps you'd like to go get something to eat, since you missed lunch?" He held his hands behind his back, which would've made any other man seem gentlemanly, but with *this* man, she wanted his hands in sight.

Professor Cook cleared his throat. "Mr. Oleson, perhaps you've forgotten your job?" His dark bushy eyebrows arched over darker penetrating eyes.

"Yes," she replied. "I think you've forgotten your job. I'm sure I'll see you tomorrow, Mr. Oleson." The name felt so strange on her tongue. Though she couldn't claim she'd spoken to him often, he'd always been *Barton*. She gathered everything from her desk and followed Izzy from the room.

Why did her heart clatter so? It was just Barton, but something about the way he looked at her now made her heart race. He made her nervous, that had to be it. Though, he'd always made her nervous, this feeling was wholly different.

"Land sakes." Izzy wound her arm around Lula's. "I couldn't believe my eyes when Barton walked in the room. *My*, has he grown up." She gave a very unladylike whistle.

Lula giggled and swatted her hand. "Where in the world did you learn to do that?"

Izzy laughed, "I have as many brothers as you have sisters, remember?"

"I've heard Beau do that, put his fingers to his lips. It about splits your head in two."

"My brothers whistle when they see a pretty filly, horse or otherwise." She bumped her hip against Lula's "And I figure a pretty man is no different."

"Barton is *not* pretty," she

protested, but it was almost a lie. While he wasn't pretty, somehow, over the three months they'd been apart, he'd turned into a man. And a handsome one at that. If he wasn't such a pest, she could admit it. *But he is a pest, and don't forget it...*

"Oh, sure he's not. I know you don't like him. He's always been so awful to you, but he sure wasn't today. In fact, he seemed quite cozy when he was talking with you."

Lula felt heat rush up her cheeks, she'd hoped no one had noticed. "He wants to start over. I don't think I can."

Izzy stopped and yanked Lula to a stop as well. "What about all that forgiveness you talked about last year when Agatha stole Marty from me? I was hurt, I loved Marty. You said that if he asks for forgiveness, I should give it to him. Doesn't that apply to you, too?"

Lula sighed. It was always so much easier to give advice than take it. Having seven sisters, she was always getting well-meaning advice, but she hadn't realized she'd been guilty of giving it, too. "I know you're right. I do forgive him, but I just don't want to start over. I don't want a friendship with him. I didn't even want to see him."

"Then you haven't really forgiven, not by what you said to me. If he's ready to be sorry for all the things he did, then accept it and let him be kind to you in the future. What have you got to lose? He's the teacher's assistant. You might even get better grades."

Lula groaned. "Don't say that. Now I'll wonder if I got the marks I did because I earned it, or because Barton wants me to be nice."

"Maybe he wants a little more than that. He sure had eyes just for you when he walked in this morning." She batted her long dark lashes. "You just wait Lula. I bet that man has plans for you."

"I want nothing to do with anything he's planning. I need to go get something to eat, I'll meet you back in the room." Lula scrambled from Izzy, tired of the conversation. Would Barton dominate the whole day? Couldn't she just enjoy anything? The cafeteria was closed in preparation for supper, but one woman took pity on her and sent her off with a thick slice of bread. The scents from the kitchen made her empty stomach grumble. She was ready for a meal, not just a snack. She nibbled on it as she walked the hallway back toward the dorm.

"I'm glad you were able to get something."

Lula jumped and spun around as Barton approached her from behind. His warm blue eyes scanned her whole face, but lingered on her lips for a moment longer than they should've.

"Yes, well. I missed the noon meal. I...wasn't feeling well and went to lie down."

His taut masculine lips pulled back into a smile. "You're a terrible liar, Lula. We both know you ran away to escape me and you changed your clothes and hair because you think I haven't changed from when you knew me before. I haven't had a chance yet to prove to you that I have. But, I will."

He held out his elbow and tipped his head. Such a gentlemanly thing to do. The second time that day he'd *appeared* the gentleman. What could he possibly want? She took the bait and prayed she wouldn't regret it, but Izzy was right. Forgiveness meant she had to at least try to hear him out. She took his arm and he directed them down the hall toward the door.

"Why, Barton, I mean, Mr. Oleson, is it so important for you to have my forgiveness?"

He stopped them and stared into her very soul. "Because I worked harder than I've ever worked before to have the chance to ask for that one thing. It means everything to me."

"Everything?" she choked. "But I told you in class, I don't want to start a new friendship with you, yet here you are."

"And you haven't walked away yet. I spent two years chasing you, trying to get your attention. I went about it all wrong, and like I said in the class, I'm sorry about that. I'm done chasing you, thinking it will draw you closer to me." He stepped nearer, his breath a caress on her cheek. "I will show you the man I am, honorable and true, and then you can either keep running away, or fall into my arms." His eyes pierced hers with a heat like she'd never known. "I'll be here to catch you."

That evening, Barton scrubbed his hands through his hair and groaned, slamming his hand on his paper-strewn desk. He'd played his whole hand, laid the cards on the table. Now she'd run from him for sure. But he couldn't help it. He'd looked into those deep blue eyes of hers and seen nothing but fear, distrust. What if she packed up and went home, or reported him to one of the other teachers? Not that they'd ever listened to her before, thank the Lord. If they had, he'd have gotten the expulsion he deserved instead of just a sore bottom and long talk with his pa. While the tanning had faded quickly, Pa's words hadn't. *You treat a lady with respect at all times, never cause her discomfort, never embarrass her publicly. And, if you ever get married, always, always have your disagreements in private. Not only are arguments a private matter, working them out afterword is better done alone.*

The boy he'd been would've purposely looked for a fight, just to make up, but now, he was a man who would never wish a fight just to get closer to his gal. Lula had seen enough of his bad side for a good long time.

Frank, the teacher he shared his quarters with, strode in and closed the door behind him with a dramatic sigh. "How I hate the first day back. The students are so excited and noisy. It's impossible to have a good day." He pushed away from the door and shrugged out of his suit coat. "There was one little boy that just wouldn't behave, pestering every student. I don't like to discipline on the first day, but if he doesn't quiet down by tomorrow..."

Barton's temper rose by degrees. "Give him a chance. He's probably new to the school. They don't always have the same rules as we do in the small country schools."

Frank sat down in the one padded rocker in the room. "I'm sure he'll be fine by tomorrow. I don't want to have to do anything. Perhaps walking around the grounds to get to know everything would be a good way to get rid of the useless energy."

"I like useless energy. I have a question for you. Is Professor Cook against his assistants talking to the students? Twice today he took me to task for talking when he wasn't teaching." He moved some of the papers around on his desk so Frank wouldn't look too far into the question. No one but Lula need ever find out his true purpose for being there, and only Lula *after* he was sure she was his.

Frank sat forward in his seat. "Hmmm. I don't know that I had that trouble. I didn't really wish to speak to the students. They were younger than me and none of them had the intention to stay here, so making their acquaintance would've been strange. Not to mention that, as the assistant, you have to grade their papers. It wouldn't do for you to have favorites in any way. It might even force the professor to fail the student."

Barton couldn't ever let that happen. He'd hurt Lula enough. If he ruined her chances of being a teacher, she'd never forgive him. He'd never forgive himself. "But, has that ever happened? Surely assistants and students talk? They are only a year apart in most cases and, in my case, my age."

Frank's face set in a serious frown. "You're going to have to throw off those friendships or risk their future, and yours. You're only an assistant, if they find you getting too friendly with a student, it wouldn't be hard to show that you were helping them. Don't do it."

Barton turned from Frank and scribbled on the top of his papers. There had to be a way to make sure the professor graded Lula's paper's so that even if his intentions were discovered, it would be him that was taken to task, and not her. Every scheme he'd had involving her had always been to make sure she was caught and not him, now he had to ensure the opposite.

Frank stood and laid a hand on his shoulder. "They might be a little lenient if, at the very least, you stay away from the women. Don't even look at them. Once you get out into the world and teaching at a school, you're allowed to dally and even marry, which is more than school boards allow women teachers, but not here. Be thankful you're a man. Teaching needs to be the only thing you think about. Professor Cook would rather you be so engrossed in the work that he gives you that you forget to eat, than for you to find extra time to talk."

Barton tapped his pencil on the desk loudly to stop Frank's words. He didn't want to hear any more. How could he possibly show Lula he'd changed if he couldn't speak to her, couldn't be seen with her... It was hopeless. He'd done all the work of becoming a teacher for nothing.

"I guess if Professor Cook already said something to you, but didn't speak to you or discipline you, maybe he no longer feels that way. But it's only been eight years since I was in his class and he made it quite clear then."

If he had to keep Lula a secret, he'd just have to get her off the school grounds and make sure no one saw them coming or going together. He'd managed for the last two years to do anything he pleased right under the teacher's nose and not get caught. Now, he just needed that luck to be with him for one more year.

Chapter Five

Lula sat in her dorm room in front of the mirror. Did she wear her hair up because of Barton, or down, the way she wanted to? Izzy came up behind her and took the brush from her hands, gently working the knots from the back.

"I can see why you always wore it up. It's so curly, it must get snarled easily. Want me to do it for you?"

Lula reached back and took the brush. "Thank you, no. I think I might try leaving it down today."

"You tried that yesterday and it bothered you so badly you missed lunch. You can't do that again. It's just not healthy."

And living her life in fear of what one man might do wasn't either. "I didn't miss lunch because I thought my hair would snarl. I left because I was worried Barton would go after my hair. He tugged on it the very first thing when he came in yesterday."

Izzy sat on the end of her own bed and cocked her head. "Well, isn't that a strange thing for a teacher to do, especially one who antagonized you so."

Lula's heart fluttered. Izzy was right, it was strange. "I don't understand why or how, just that he did. That's why I left to put my hair up. To remove the temptation for him to tease me further." It hadn't worked. Her heart raced even now at his words, *I will show you the man I am, honorable and true, and then you can either keep running away, or fall into my arms. I'll be here to catch you.*

"And you changed your skirt. You really think he'd risk his internship to tease you? I don't think he would. They only give those to very capable students, he'd be a fool to risk it. And, despite how he's always treated you, he was a good student in primary...for a boy."

But he was risking his internship, wasn't he? He'd already staked his claim to her time, saying he was going to show her what kind of a man he was. Unless she'd completely misunderstood and he'd meant *as a teacher*, but the way he'd leaned in and lowered his voice had given the impression he had something much more personal in mind.

"Down or up, you'd best hurry. We don't want to be late." Izzy turned to go to her own trunk at the foot of her bed. "Frankly, I'm not fond of the fact that we all look the same all the time. I liked the first day where we wore our best clothes. Now, all the ladies will wear the same black skirts and white shirts. No color. What's wrong with a lavender walking suit? Nothing, that's what. Some schools even tell you how many petticoats you must wear. It's ridiculous. I think they want all of us to be boring before we ever see a classroom as a teacher. I'm surprised they don't tell us how often we must bathe." Izzy raked her brush through her hair.

Izzy had a fire that Lula wished she had. When she'd first come to Spearfish Normal, she'd had the same mischievous streak as Izzy, but it had died quickly as she'd tried to remain invisible. It hadn't worked. Nothing had helped her evade the boy that had plagued her. "You may be more than Professor Cook is bargaining for, Izzy. What are you going to do for the essay he assigned? I know you have your own theories on teaching and they aren't what he sounded like he wanted to hear."

Izzy braided her hair and wrapped it into a sturdy knot at her nape. She arched her neck perfectly and placed a book on her head, taking even steps across the room. "Just like any good student can do for me, I am capable of reciting just what the teacher wants to hear." She let the book fall, catching it before it hit the floor. "But, you're right. I do have my own mind and when I have my own class, I'll put those things into practice."

The emptiness that had slowly seeped into her veins over the summer crept a little closer to her heart. While the other girls had visions of standing in front of a class, she'd lost that vision, that fire. "I wish I could be there to see it. It's almost a shame that they don't let two teachers work together. It would make teaching students so much easier." Lula twisted her curls around her fingers to tighten them, since she didn't have time to heat an iron. Despite what Izzy had said, she wanted to look good, better than any of the others in the room. She wasn't ready to accept Barton's direct attention, but the warmth of his regard felt good.

Her sisters, Ruby, Jennie, Hattie, Eva, and Frances had all married. When they got together, they spoke of sweet feelings and stolen kisses when no one was looking. Strong arms that held them all night. *Barton has strong arms...* Lula clenched her eyes shut and banished the thought. It was only his talk yesterday that left her thinking such strange things. That had to be his new game, to try to make her insides feel wobbly, then he'd laugh at her. There had to be some way he could embarrass or hurt her, he couldn't have changed that much.

She stood and went to her own chest at the end of her bed. As Izzy had said, everyone would now be wearing dark skirts with white shirts. Anyone who wanted to stand out a little could wear a tie, but most wouldn't. The women in the Normal School courses all wanted the same thing, to graduate without making a name for themselves. Going outside of what was expected would be disastrous. She slipped her own dark skirt over her head and fastened it shut, swishing it so it fell properly with her petticoats.

"Izzy, I do think it's time for class."

Izzy gave an impish grin. "I think it's time to go see the teacher's assistant."

Only a fool would continue. That's what Barton kept telling himself. He'd been a fool to waste his whole summer doing training he didn't care about and now he was a fool to try to see Lula when it could destroy everything he'd done so far. But, hadn't he convinced his pa to let him come and do this, to make it right? Didn't he owe it to his pa and to himself to try? So, that made him a fool. He'd accept the name.

Lula was worth it. But he had to consider how to keep his place long enough to convince her to give him a chance *and* make sure that *she* didn't lose *her* place. If she did, all would be lost. While he, as a man, might be forgiven a little indiscretion, she wouldn't be. Her career would be over and it would be all his fault. He'd done enough destroying where she was concerned.

The campus was already buzzing with students making their way about to either breakfast or to class to get in some quiet study time. The exception would be the primary students, though they were kept separated from the adult students. He carried a stack of papers fresh from the new mimeograph machine and kept away from the other students walking the paths. If he got to class early, got everything perfectly ready for Cook, he would have no reason to look deeper into his interest in Lula. But, just to be safe, he wouldn't approach her in class anymore.

The clock struck the half hour as he entered the dark classroom. The thick white pull shades kept the sun and afternoon heat out, but needed to be opened in the morning for light. He made quick work of pulling them up, then stacked the papers on the professor's desk and finally, set about writing that day's notes on the board. So far, learning to teach had been little more than following the orders of the professor, but after the Christmas holiday, the teaching would be on his shoulders. A syllabus was available for him to use, but he'd have to create his own lectures from it, and his own homework. He'd also have to grade all the papers, as if he really were the teacher.

He arranged the desks and chairs in perfect order, then held his breath as he looked to the clock again. She'd be arriving any minute. Lula was always punctual and kind, except when someone pushed her too far. Her words cut through the years as if he were still the boy standing behind the school with buttery fingers. *I hate you Barton Oleson!* Could he overcome two years of bad behavior and a hatred built up over time and circumstance? He'd roped cows, busted horses, and raised cane with his brothers, but atoning for the hurt he'd done to Lula was a harder toil than any of the other chores had been. And so much more depended on it.

A few other students came in and he nodded to them in welcome. Most didn't pay him much mind and that was fine. He wasn't there to make friends with any of them. Some would pass the class, others wouldn't, but they weren't his concern. Except for one. Two female students bustled in, chatting away. One batted her lashes at him. He chuckled to himself. That one might not last long, since both of them were only a year away from the age of their oldest students. She would have to decide which was more important, continuing her education, or looking for a mate. The current theories on teaching didn't allow for married teachers unless they worked with their husbands, and though a few schools were breaking with that tradition, they were few.

The clock ticked ever closer to eight when the professor would come and start class. Lula and Izzy only had two minutes to make it in and get seated or they'd be counted as late. He couldn't lie to cover for her. The attendance log sat out in front of him and he made a check mark by two more students as they walked in. Where was she? His pulse quickened. Had she abandoned the school when he'd been so plain about his intentions? Could she have run when he needed her to stay put?

One more minute. His finger itched to mark her as present. He glanced to the door, praying she hadn't left and that she would swing in any moment. He suddenly felt like he'd been up for far longer than the two hours it had taken to get to eight o'clock. Just as the minute hand struck the twelve, Lula and Izzy walked into class and silently shuffled to their seats.

Relief flooded him so fast, he nearly fell from the rush to his head. She wasn't gone and he could mark her as on time. Barely. He sighed as Professor Cook strode into the room and closed the door behind him. Barton cloaked his face with a teacher's rigid mask and said another prayer that he'd find a minute to talk to Lula later.

Chapter Six

Lula deliberately slowed her steps as she approached the classroom. Her skin tingled to life. Barton would be inside, preparing for class. She couldn't go in until she was sure he'd have no time to talk to her, to persuade her. Because what if he tried to change her? Could she ever trust him, wasn't his word completely tainted by his past? He'd hurt her day after day, without care. In fact, he'd reveled in it. He'd turned the teachers against her, and some students, too. His taunting had encouraged others to take part and she'd soon earned the awful name Lousy Lula. *He'd* never called her that but it didn't matter, the name he'd chosen had been even worse, Buttercup, after he'd slathered her with it.

What would he say or do today to try to convince her that he was a changed man, if indeed he was? Would he be as obvious as he'd been the day before, talking to her, leaning over her desk? She tucked her curls behind her ear and bit her lip. As much as she prayed he was reformed, she didn't want him coming around her, testing her judgment of him. Just seeing him set her on edge and made her want to run. But hadn't he said he'd be there to catch her? Well, he certainly thought highly of himself, but hadn't he always?

As she waited, Izzy touched her shoulder startling her from her thoughts. "You can't just stay out here. They'll mark you absent and you only get two of those before you get expelled. Get inside. We've only got one minute to spare."

Her lungs didn't seem to work quite right as she pushed herself to walk through the door and there, front and center, stood Barton. His crisp white shirt was bright against his tan face and snug against his shoulders. How did a man who'd studied all summer long still get kissed by the sun? She almost lost the fight not to giggle at her thoughts. A man like him wouldn't pass up getting kissed by anything. She rushed to her seat and took it at the last moment.

The professor stormed in and cleared his throat, dismissing Barton with a quick wave. Barton came around the desk and his gaze met hers for just a moment, sending heat up her cheeks and down to her belly, before he settled in right in front of her. The collar of his shirt sat right along the bottom edge of his sandy brown hair. Hair that looked much softer than a man's should, like he spent time preening it. Most men didn't seem to care much for grooming, always covering their heads with a hat or slapping their hair full of pomade, but Barton's was clean and neat. Orderly and trimmed. Exactly what Barton had never been, or maybe he had and she'd just never noticed. She'd been too afraid of him to care.

The professor's voice droned on. She sighed and tried to pay attention, but having *him* so close left her wary and tense. Even in front of her with no way for him to attack, he made her blood rush. Barton tensed at the sound of her sigh, his shoulders bunching with muscles that were usually invisible under his tailored white shirts. What could be bothering him? She'd already lost all concentration in the class, unable to pay any attention when he was around. His threat to woo her, such as it was, was having the effect he'd desired. She couldn't stop thinking about it, or him. Or what he might do next.

Chalk screeched across the chalkboard and she shuddered back into the class. Izzy had a handout on her desk and was feverishly writing on it. Lula looked down and saw a copy on her own desk and realized it had been handed to her at some point while she'd been distracted and she hadn't paid the slightest attention. Professor Cook wiped the board with his left hand as he wrote with his right and any chance she may have had to catch up with the class was lost to the dust that choked the front of the room.

Professor Cook turned to the class. "And that, students, was the conclusion I want you to come to as you look at writing your essays. Be sure to include every point discussed in today's lecture. You're dismissed for the day to work on it."

The blank lines in purple mimeo ink on the handout taunted her. How had she let her mind wander for so long that she'd missed an entire lecture which would determine much of her grade for the first nine weeks of class? Izzy sighed next to her and flung her pencil to the desk as she massaged her palm. "I hope you got some good notes. I did my best to keep up, but my hand cramped near the end and I missed the last one." She smiled and blew a wisp of hair from her temple.

Lula couldn't admit that she'd been distracted, not with her distraction sitting too close to hear. He'd think he'd won and she'd never let him have that satisfaction. He could woo her until his dying breath and she'd still say no. She had to say no. Not only would it be impossible to fall for such a horrid man, but she had to stay single to be a teacher. There was no other way. So, whether his arms were open and willing or not—not that she cared—he couldn't catch her. There was no two ways about it.

"I'll show you my notes when we get back to the room." She shoved her paper into her book and slapped it shut. The clock was to the left of the door and she craned around to see that it was only nine in the morning. It had only been one hour since they'd arrived. She whipped around and stood, realizing her folly. Barton couldn't be given the chance to talk to her, but she was left standing, looking around. He'd disappeared. When she'd been talking to Izzy or looking at the clock, he'd left to clean the board with the awful smelling cleaner. And though he was only a few yards away, his back was to her and he was busy. He hadn't even wished her a good morning...

It should've been a cause for rejoicing. Maybe he'd given up. But she didn't. He'd said he was going to pursue her, and had since ignored her. Wasn't she worth the time or effort? He was so confusing and her desire to watch him walk away but also to come talk to her warred within her.

Izzy gathered everything off her desk. "Lula, come on. We've got so much work to do. He gave so much information today. I don't know how we're going to fit it all in." Izzy grabbed her about the arm and yanked her toward the door. "Don't worry about Mr. Oleson, he'll still be there after Thursday."

Heat rushed to her face as Barton's arm stopped wiping at the board. He glanced over his shoulder, his cool blue eyes met hers for a moment. He cocked a smile at Izzy's words. Oh yes, he would definitely be there after Thursday, and he hadn't given up.

The dust from the chalkboard choked him worse than the cleaner did. At least if he ever found himself in the position of being an actual teacher, he'd find a student to do that job. And the only way his Lula would let him teach, were if she were in a family way and couldn't. His heart trembled at the thought. He'd been ready for her heart for two years. It might have been a boyish infatuation, but now, at eighteen, it was anything but. Even the thought of children with her excited him.

Izzy said his name and he glanced over his shoulder to catch Lula drinking him in, and he couldn't help but smile. He hadn't spoken a word to her yet that day, but she was thinking about him. Her soft sigh during class, her gentle breath over the back of his neck, had made concentration difficult. So difficult, in fact, that he'd missed when the professor had asked him to hand out some papers and had resorted to just having the students take one and pass it on.

Professor Cook approached him and rested a hand on his shoulder. "Barton, I know we've expected a lot of you the past few months. You've done an excellent job, none of us could complain. But you must complete this year and I can't expect any less of you just because of the short time you chose to complete the task. You assured me and the rest of the staff that you could do this. Have you changed your mind?"

His hand on the chalkboard slowed to a stop. The professor had to be thinking of his missed cue to hand out the papers, he hadn't neglected any other job. "I'm sorry about this morning. I was thinking through how I would re-write my own paper and missed your question. I won't let my mind slip again. What's done is done, my grades earned."

A smile touched the mustachioed

teacher and he patted Barton on the shoulder. "You did a fine job on all of your assignments. No need to worry a bit about your past work. Think only of your future now. It's very close. When you complete this year, I have no doubt I'll be writing you a glowing recommendation to wherever you want to teach. It's good to see one so driven that they would give up a summer to get ahead."

There was no way to answer the professor. He hadn't done it to get ahead in *his* career, but to get ahead of *hers*. If he'd been on equal footing with Lula, she could ignore him. But she couldn't ignore a teacher, couldn't ignore him now. "I won't forget, sir. And thank you again for taking time from your family to help me."

The professor ignored his gratitude and left him standing in the room. Now, he had to rush to prepare notes for the next day so he could be at the cafeteria the entire time it was open. There were precious few times he could get away with talking to Lula out and about, and after mealtime was one of them. He wouldn't miss her. He'd had to remain silent during class, so he didn't alert the suspicion of the professor or any of the other students, but he couldn't go a whole day without talking to her.

If he could catch up with her, there had to be somewhere he could ask to meet her, somewhere they could have the privacy to talk. Spearfish had a bustling boardwalk with blocks of hardware stores, post office, livery, and black smith...none of which would be all that interesting to show Lula. Nor would it tempt her to leave the school campus.

Frank popped his head in the doorway and waved. "Still here? I heard Cook let you out early. Figured you'd take the afternoon to go riding. Weren't you just complaining that the weather would turn before you got the chance to take that nag of yours out?"

Star wasn't a nag, but he let the insult pass as Frank had given him a fantastic idea. He could rent another horse and he and Lula could ride to one of the nearby falls, Bridal Veil or Rough Lock. He'd let her pick. Students wouldn't make the jaunt out there, so they wouldn't be seen, but there would be enough visitors that they wouldn't exactly be alone, either. It was perfect. He just had to convince Lula.

Chapter Seven

Their small dorm room wouldn't hold Izzy's anger. "What do you mean you didn't get any notes?" Izzy clutched her cheeks. "What will we do? I didn't get everything. He erased it too quickly... There has to be someone else who got all the notes. She whipped around and paced back and forth in the narrow space between their beds.

If Izzy continued, Lula would have to leave. Pacing always left her with a headache. "I'm sorry, Izzy. It's just…he was sitting right there in front of me and I couldn't even think straight." It sounded like the poor excuse it was.

"And just how do you intend to pass your courses if you can't keep your head?

He didn't say a word to you. This is a hard course and we need each other. We both promised each other two years ago that we'd go through this together. Are you still with me?"

Through all the messes and all the tears of the past two years, Izzy had been faithful, the best of friends. "I'm sorry, Izzy. I'll sit further back in the row and then he won't be near me. I won't let him distract me any further. Let's see what you got, maybe the other point is in one of the text books. It's a good thing he gave us this whole day to work on it."

Izzy resumed her pacing. "What if it isn't? I should go and talk to one of the other students. Ask them."

It would do no good for Lula to look when Izzy had written down most of the items and would recognize those from her notes. She could look through the texts and find the other points easier. "No, you stay here. It's my fault we're missing the last one. You go ahead and look through the books. I'll go ask the other students. They might be in the library."

A flash of anger crossed Izzy's face. "You'd better not get distracted. If he's there you *will not* speak to him."

There wasn't really a chance she would. Barton would be off doing something for Cook, so she didn't have to worry. "I won't. I'll just go to the library, copy the notes from one of the other students, and come right back. We can spend our evening writing our papers. Tomorrow we can each read through them and then they should be perfect to turn in."

Izzy visibly calmed at the detailed plan. Despite her need to be social on occasion, Izzy preferred structure and placidity. Lula had always appreciated that both of them were happiest with one friend: each other. Izzy handed her a notepad and pencil with a stern look. She didn't require more.

The room emptied to a long hallway of doors, all leading to identical small rooms. Each housed two girls. The walls in both the halls and dorms where white, or had been when they'd been first painted. Lula strode down the hall, keeping a look out for the other girls in her class. If they were about, her search would be over quickly.

No one roamed between her door and the exit and soon she pushed the doors out into the wide courtyard between the women's dorm and the administration building. Most students were still in class, so the grounds were empty. A large bushy hedge sat at the corner of the Administration building and as Lula strode by she was yanked behind it with a screech, her heart racing. Barton stood there, covering his lips with a finger.

"Barton!" she managed, though her heart was stuck in her throat.

He covered her mouth with his hand, quickly sending a surge through her she'd never felt before, then gave her a quelling look, finally dropping his fingers. Here it was, he was always ready to attack her, he'd just had to wait to catch her unawares. She took a step back to get out of the hedge.

He grasped her arm and tugged her back into the wall of his chest. Now she really couldn't breathe.

She lowered her voice to a squeak, "Just what do you think you're doing besides frightening me? Yet again." Hadn't he promised to stop, though this was different than any of his other teasing behavior. He'd never done anything in private, had never been allowed a moment alone with her.

His chuckle built a fire in her chest as he let her step back a pace. "I was waiting here to scare unsuspecting underclassman."

"I don't doubt it!" She hissed as she backed away a little more, hoping to break free of the bush and get back to her task. He reached for her and caught her arm, holding her fast this time.

"Do you really think so little of me, Lula?" Those blue eyes had tricked her before, but now, there was earnest hurt in their depths.

After so long, she couldn't give up being wary of him. It was second nature. She brushed his hand away. "I thought I'd make it through a whole day unscathed. You didn't speak a word to me in class."

A brief whisper of triumph lit his eyes, then he hid it. "You came in too late, and I had work to do. Strictly speaking, I'm not allowed to have any sort of relationship with my students. It...wouldn't be proper."

Just what kind of relationship was he hoping for? "If that is the case, then why do you keep trying to start one? Are you trying to get me expelled? Because I know from experience that *you* won't accept any fault if we were discovered. No matter how much it would be deserved." She crossed her arms over her chest, feeling exposed in front of him.

"We never would've gotten caught if you hadn't been so persistent in trying to get me into trouble." His grin was more than infuriating. How could he think for a second she would ever want to put up with all the trouble he'd dealt her?

"And just what was I supposed to do, Barton? Allow you to bully me further? You used to distract me from studies, kept me from going outdoors, forced me to wear my hair one way, and clothing that would never show stains. I let you control every part of me, how else could I fight back?" Blasted tears. She'd shed enough for this man.

He touched her cheek and drew away in the next heartbeat. "Oh, Lula. I never knew. I just wanted..." He sucked in a deep breath. "It doesn't matter now. You have to let me make it up to you. I won't get you in trouble and if you ever report me, I'll take the full blame. I will go home and take the shame of it. Just please, give me the chance to make it right. Give me the chance to start fresh."

His words kindled a hope within her, that she could complete the year of studies without worry. Barton wouldn't stand in her way. He wouldn't play any tricks on her or get her labeled a troublemaker. "Barton, I…"

He held up his hand. "As much as I love hearing my name on your lips, you can't get used to calling me that. If we are ever caught, they would see our familiarity. I would like the chance to talk to you away from the school, away from any chance that you and I could be seen. I'll be taking a ride in Spearfish this afternoon. Would you care to join me?"

A ride? He wanted her to join him away from the school? What sort of pleasant adventure would the son of a cattle baron plan? The little voice in the back of her mind reminded her that if she planned to succeed, she couldn't ever marry. But Barton wasn't asking to court her. He wasn't looking for a wife, he wanted forgiveness. Going along with him wouldn't be leading his heart down a path she could never let him complete, because they both had the same goal. Teaching. A teacher couldn't marry. She bit her lip and tried to think of all the reasons she shouldn't go, and came up short.

However, the notebook, still resting in her arms, was all the reminder she needed. Closing her eyes to keep her true desires from being seen, she replied, "I'm sorry, Mr. Oleson. As much as I love riding. I can't. I have to write my paper tonight. I'm sure you understand."

As she opened her eyes, the understanding in his was almost too much to bear. He wasn't angry or hurt, emotions she'd been used to giving others when she didn't get her way. Maybe he had matured more than she'd given him credit for.

"Promise me you'll consider going this weekend, after the paper is turned in?" He leaned against the building next to her shoulder, relaxed and hopeful.

Why did he have to make it so difficult? Why did his eyes tempt her to trust him? This was Barton, the man she absolutely *did not want* to spend time with. The boy who she'd foolishly prayed would somehow get in trouble for his misdeeds or at the very least not show up for school after each break. She shouldn't be considering his request, she should be laughing at him and running the other direction. He held her future in his hands. If they were caught, despite what he said, his past said he wouldn't take the blame, she would.

His soft blue eyes pled with her. "Lula? Miss Arnsby? Please?"

She'd been hearing an awful lot of please from him the last few days. A word she'd never heard from him before. Could a man really go through such a drastic change? A mountaintop experience might do it. Lula took a deep breath. "All right. I'll take a ride with you."

A smile bright enough to blot the sun broke over his face. "You won't regret it."

Lula nodded and dashed from behind the bush. The lack of regret remained to be seen.

That night, Lula lay on the floor, facing Izzy. Both had their notebooks out and pages upon pages of writing for their essays spread out in front of them. A lamp cast its glow just far enough for them both to see well enough to continue. They should've been in bed hours before, but the drive to finish with a satisfactory grade was strong.

"It was good that Lawson allowed you to copy his notes." Izzy tapped her pencil to her lips cutting into the silence. "There was no way to finish the paper without it. None of the books had anything close to his lecture points."

Lula ran her finger down her paper, making sure all the arguments had been mentioned. "It was. Though, I forgot to mention. You owe him an afternoon at the ice cream shop for the use of his notes." Izzy's silence forced her glance from her paper to her friend's look of mortification. Lula couldn't stifle a laugh, even with the fatigue pressing down on her. "At least he's handsome and doesn't have Cook's mustache." She draped her fingers over her top lip and wiggled them to mimic their professor's abundance of facial hair.

"You're serious? Why didn't he ask you? You were the one getting his notes." Izzy pretended interest in her paper, but the fact that she was looking at Lula's upside-down notes, gave her away.

Lula chuckled, remembering Lawson's embarrassment as she'd approached him in the library. He hadn't been interested in her in the slightest, not that she would've agreed to those terms for herself, anyway. Lawson knew her as *Izzy's friend*, which was just fine. "Funny thing. He couldn't remember my name, but had no trouble remembering yours. It couldn't hurt to spend one evening out."

Izzy sat up, wiping her hands down her skirt, and regarded her with a serious line to her lips. "That's where you're wrong, Lula. What if I found that I liked him after just one outing? It wouldn't matter for him. He can get married and still teach, but not so for me. If I get married, all the work I've done so far, all my dreams...would be over. While starting a family and being the good and dutiful wife might be pleasant for some, I want more. I may have joked with you about Barton's plans for you, but that's all it was, useless joking. You can't and I can't, because what we're doing here, studying now, matters."

It was true. She wanted more too, but how could Izzy find out something so life-changing over one scoop of ice cream? And, would it be the same with one horse ride? No, never. Barton might have turned his life around, might offer her sweet words, but her heart couldn't be softened to him. They'd already shared more talk than Izzy would in a short trip to the druggist and her heart hadn't been swayed so far.

"I don't think I'd pass up the ice cream. It's just an afternoon, and how often will you get to have such a treat?"

"But would you really take that chance? Could you ever be happy teaching if your heart was only half in it? If you were constantly wondering about what you might have given up? My heart can't be changed as quickly as a dress, but I would know if he was a potential for me after just one outing. If I felt drawn to him, liked his company, and had to stop seeing him because

I could see myself with him...my heart would forever be torn in two. I can't risk that. Could you?"

Chapter Eight

It was harder to be distracted by Barton when Lula sat in the back, as she'd promised Izzy. Almost harder than it was to ignore her promise just to listen to a few words from him. After agreeing to go riding with him, her attention had been razor sharp on turning in her paper on time, and with perfection. But on Friday, where there had been no paper to consume her, nor was lecture all that interesting, her mind had wandered. All the way to the front of the room and a well-groomed teacher's assistant. How strange to think of *him* and not a means of escape!

Riding with Barton would be a nice get away from the strain of school, of hours poring over papers and facts that made little sense before she ever stood in front of a class. She'd always done her riding at the ranch, and always on the same horse. Would he consider her a poor horsewoman if she couldn't hold her own? She just prayed he secured a placid horse, not one too spirited.

Far ahead of her, Barton stood and made his way around the room handing out mimeographed pages. He'd left her alone the last two days while she'd finished her paper, but now she was dying to know where she should meet him or if he still wanted to take her at all. He took pages off the top of the stack for everyone until he made it to her desk, then he flipped to the bottom of his sheaf of remaining pages and handed her the one on the bottom, continuing on with hardly a glance.

No one else would notice his slight hesitation at her desk, but because she'd been watching his every movement, it was apparent to her. The page was thicker than it ought to be and she flipped it over to find a second page. It had only a brief note in pencil: *Meet me by the bridge, tomorrow, 1:00. We'll walk to town for the horses, then ride to Bridal Veil Falls. B*

There was a moment of hesitation in her heart that she released immediately. What did Izzy know of matters of the heart? Lula wasn't going to get entangled with Barton, it was only fun. Just a little ride to the falls. When would she have a chance to see them otherwise? This was her third year in Spearfish and she'd never even been into the town. Until now, she'd been too young to set out on her own. But she was an adult now, and could make her own choice.

Izzy glanced at her and tipped her head in question. How would she convince Izzy it was a good idea to go...with the teacher's assistant? The closest thing to the teacher. Forbidden in so many ways. Izzy would never agree to remain silent about it. She would advise her against it and probably sit in front of the door to keep her from making such a choice, but she'd be doing it as a friend, thinking she had better judgment. Over the next day, she'd have to think of a good excuse, or risk Izzy's questions.

Her stomach twisted at the idea of lying to her friend. If there was any way to go about it without telling her a lie, she would. Izzy opened her mouth to say something as Mr. Lawson arrived next to her. Izzy clamped her mouth firmly shut.

Lula attempted a pleasant smile while holding in her laughter at her poor friend. "Good afternoon, Mr. Lawson."

He gave Lula a nod, but turned to Izzy almost immediately. "Miss Harmon, I'd be pleased if you would join me this weekend to try out the new ice cream machine at the druggist in Spearfish." He waited, stiff with embarrassment.

Izzy glanced to Lula with wide eyes. It was one thing to refuse Mr. Lawson's offer when it had been Lula posing it, but could she refuse him to his face? Mr. Lawson had a quiet, reserved demeanor that might not make someone immediately notice him. But now that he was here and waiting on Izzy, Lula could call him handsome with his dark hair and eyes, too afraid to smile.

As he became more uncomfortable by the moment, Izzy chewed on her lip and seemed to be at a loss for words. Lula cleared her throat as delicately as she was able. "Mr. Lawson, Miss Harmon is a little shy. Perhaps if you invited a few friends with you, she might be more willing to go? Say, tomorrow at one o'clock?" Oh, how wicked she felt, tossing Izzy into a situation she knew Izzy wouldn't want. Izzy flipped around in her chair and pegged her with an angry glare.

Mr. Lawson smiled and sighed as if she'd just given him the answer to all the world's problems. "That would be no trouble at all. My friend Amos and his girl Molly would love to join us. Would you do me the honor, Miss Harmon?"

Izzy took a deep breath and Lula prayed she wouldn't say anything but yes. "I will go with you once, because I was so grateful for your help on Wednesday. After that, I won't be able to. Because of the teaching program, I have to remain away from any type of male friends. I'm sure you understand."

Those words rang in Lula's memory. She'd said the same thing to Barton and he'd understood. Mr. Lawson's face faltered for just a moment and he took a step back. "Of...course, Miss Harmon." He ducked his head. "I'll meet you out in the courtyard after lunch tomorrow. Looking forward to it," he mumbled as he backed away.

The room emptied out of the other students and the professor, quickly leaving Lula to deal with Izzy's anger. Izzy tossed her pencil at Lula's head. "You knew how I felt about going out to ice cream. Why did you encourage him? He's nice, and handsome. I'll look silly and if he shows me any attention at all, my heart will just melt. My mama warned me about the attentions of handsome men."

"But what if you don't? What if you just like his company and he turns into a good friend. Someone else you can lean on?"

If only Ruby had given her the same warnings, of course, she wouldn't have heeded them. Barton hadn't become truly handsome until he'd become forbidden. When he was a scamp, he hadn't seemed handsome in the slightest. Well, perhaps not *ugly*. He'd never been ugly, but she hadn't been attracted to his looks when he'd been so awful to her. "It's a few hours, Izzy. I don't think you're going to lose yourself. And now there will be two other people there. It will be a fun outing."

"An outing with a couple and me and Mr. Lawson!" Izzy sighed and flopped her head over her arms on the desk. "I wonder who Molly is, she can't be a teaching student, but what other programs are offered to female students?"

Neither of them had ever considered any of the other options, as few as they were. Only teaching had interested them both. "I'm not sure. Now you'll have something to ask her."

Izzy sat up, rolled her eyes, then stood to leave. "Next time, *I'll* go get the notes and *you'll* be the one going for ice cream." She fairly growled as she dashed from the room.

Barton's voice rumbled in her ear, just behind her, and she jumped, thinking she was alone. "Ice cream? Sounds good. Who do I give my notes to for an ice cream outing with you?"

She whipped around and his grin melted her. "Do behave yourself, Mr. Oleson."

He took a step closer, his eyes found hers. "I find that I can't. No matter how hard I try. You should know that better than anyone."

The truth of his words should've been a warning, but instead she found herself holding in a giggle.

"Izzy will be out tomorrow, so she won't ask where I'm going...and with whom."

He touched her arm and she drew back. It was too soon, too fast. She couldn't fall for him. She'd enjoy his company, but she wouldn't fall into the trap Izzy was so worried about. Going with Barton would give herself a reason to forgive him, and then she'd graduate and walk away. That had to be the way of things.

He searched her face. "I can't linger here alone in the room with you, but I also must lock up. You'll have to go soon." Though his words begged her to go, his look asked her to stay and her heart raced. This was a situation that a wilder woman would wish for, but not Lula. She'd been an overly flighty child, always flitting from thing to thing, but was now well-grounded. Fancy hadn't had a bed to sleep on in her heart for a long time.

"I still don't understand why you want to spend any time at all with me. The last thing I said to you before this year, was that I hated you. I meant it then, you have to know that."

His voice vibrated just above a whisper. Utter control. "I do. I'll even agree that I deserved it. But what if I told you that every time I did anything to you in the past, it was to get the opposite reaction that you gave? I was so confused. My pa set me on the straight and narrow. I just want the chance to help you forget all that I did."

"I want to forgive you, Barton. I do. But I have so much hurt. This school was supposed to be the best thing that ever happened to me, and for two whole years, it was the worst."

"It still can be the best, Lula. I see the look in your eyes. The softening. I can't go back and fix everything I wronged, but I can try to make *this* year right for you. I can try to show you what I want to be. I was a kid then. You've got to understand that. We've both grown up since then."

She couldn't take what he was offering her. It was too easy. He'd made life horrible and now he was offering to just wipe it away like a mother wipes up spilled milk. "It's only been three months. Are you trying to convince me that you could grow up in the blink of an eye?"

He took another step closer to her and his strength surrounded her even though he wasn't touching her.

She wanted to back away but the pull to stay near him was stronger.

"I don't want you to just believe anything. I aim to prove it, and I have been. Four months ago, you wouldn't have looked me in the eye much less talk with me." He reached up and gently tugged one curl. It was so tender and, though her heart beat a crazy rhythm, it wasn't in anger. "Someday, I'll explain to you what happened that long-ago first day that sealed me as your enemy. But for now, the fact that you've stopped running, and started talking, is a small victory that I will claim." He glanced for the door. "But right now, I need you to go, before another teacher walks by and wonders why the room isn't locked...unless you want me to lock us in for a while?" He grinned.

Lula's heart tripped over itself and she gasped, grabbing for all her books and papers and spilling half of them on the floor.

He knelt down and picked them all up for her, handing them to her. "I wouldn't do that to you, Lula. I do respect you. I've got to learn that you aren't ready to relax with me yet." Hurt, mingled with heat, built in his gaze before he quelled it.

It took a minute to arrange the papers in her shaking fingers. Of course, he'd been joking. Why did she take him so seriously? He wouldn't lock them in a room alone. It would ruin his chances of them ever being teachers. But the mere thought had made her so nervous she shook. He rested his hand on her shoulder for a moment. It didn't help the quivering inside her, it sped to racing.

"Will you be alright, or did I frighten you speechless?"

She shook her head and backed away from his touch. While he *had* made her speechless, she couldn't label what she felt as fear exactly. Maybe Izzy was right. It didn't even take a whole scoop of ice cream to start questioning yourself.

Chapter Nine

Barton paced along the path just out of sight of the school. It was ten minutes to one and he'd been waiting there for a half-hour already. Too excited to eat lunch and too worried he'd see Lula in the cafeteria. He'd been able to keep from speaking to her while she'd had an assignment to think about. It *was* important, but after everything had been turned in, he'd had to be near her. And then she'd found herself alone with him in the classroom. How had he made it through full summers away from her in the past? The more she let him in, the harder it was getting to avoid her.

He turned from his path and spotted Lula descending the hill. The campus stood on a slight rise so that, from town, the tall administration building sat stalwart above all of Spearfish. Lula wore a pretty off-white skirt that wasn't a riding habit, but would be suitable. Her white, button-down shirt accentuated her narrow shoulders, and a black sash across her middle showed off her even narrower waist. He couldn't wait for that moment she finally let him wrap his hands around that waist and pull her close. But he *would* wait. He'd be a gentleman, but he'd make himself a liar if he didn't admit just seeing her made his blood run hotter.

A small smile pressed her lips into a grin as she approached. For once, he didn't feel the need to lower his voice or pretend he wasn't staring. He could look and talk all he liked. He watched her every move until she stopped in front of him.

"Why, Miss Arnsby, you look beautiful." Her smile bloomed even bigger and he stood taller under her appraising eyes, hoping she found the sight of him just as appealing.

"Barton. I think we're both smart enough to be familiar when we ought and formal when it's necessary. Not to mention, this will be our one outing. It's not something we can make a habit of, so we might as well enjoy it while we can."

Her words stopped him short and it took him a moment to collect his thoughts. "What do you mean? I had every intention of making a habit out of getting you off the school grounds as often as you'd let me." She could've just as soon slapped him over the head with a riding crop. He'd never considered that she would say no after the ride. It was meant to be the beginning, not the end. Hadn't she agreed happily to come with him? No reservations. She'd hardly even taken any time to reply when he'd asked.

"Barton. You know the rules, or maybe you never bothered to look over the parts pertaining to women. We can't go courting, and schools will not take on a teacher who is, or even who appears to be. School boards think that once women are married, we belong at home to start our own families. They don't want to deal with having to find a new teacher mid-term if we should..." She blushed a pretty crimson.

He could finish the thought...*if they were with child.* Somehow women had managed to give birth for thousands of years, but according to school boards, couldn't think straight in front of a class.

"Does this mean we're courting?" He tried to make her smile, to think of anything but the rigid rule-laden turn of her thoughts. He held out his arm and she glanced at it for a moment, taking longer to consider whether to take his arm than it had taken to say she'd come with him. Of course, maybe she really liked riding horses and that was her reason? Doubt niggled at him. He'd never had a confidence problem before, but he'd never battled two full years of bad blood before, either.

"No, Barton. We are *not* courting. I don't have that option available to me." Did he see sadness in her eyes, or was that only wishful thinking?

But she had listed it as her reason for not continuing to see him. Was it even a consideration? If she worried about marriage, was she starting to feel drawn to him? "I understand." He chose to ignore her refusal and go back to what she'd been talking about before. "If a female teacher would decide to start a family, it might make a difficult situation for the school board." But only at the end, when the baby finally came...

She nodded and took his elbow, but didn't look at him. Her cheeks still bloomed a delicate pink. He certainly didn't have to worry about whether Lula had ever been romanced by any other man. At eighteen, she had only just become a woman and was so shy and demure. To blush at the very mention of childbearing made her sweeter even than his ma's pear pie.

"So, did you agree to come with me because we're riding horses, then? I can't figure why you'd let me take you to the falls today if you'd already decided that once was enough. I'd hoped you wanted to spend a few minutes...with me." His frustration was hard to contain.

Lula squeezed his elbow. "Both," she whispered.

His feet were lighter than air and he wanted to twirl Lula around in one of the jigs his grandpap had taught him. "In that case, hold your refusal until the next time I ask. Let's not overshadow this day with thoughts like that." He pushed ahead and didn't give her the chance to argue with him. Now that she could argue back, she was quite willing to tell him just what she thought. "My pa always brings my horse, Star, with us when he brings me to school in the fall. She's down at the livery. I'm sure we can find a good horse for you there, too."

"I've only ridden one horse before. Until we moved onto the ranch in Deadwood, almost six years ago, I'd never touched a horse."

The day wouldn't go anywhere near as well as he'd planned if she couldn't ride. "But you are comfortable on a horse, right?" He could always let her sit with him on his... No, he couldn't do that. She would be far too close to him.

"Yes, I'm sure I can handle it well enough. Have you ever been down to the falls? Is there a trail?"

Thankful for the change in subject, Barton drew her down the street toward the livery. Spearfish was a wealthy town, with broad streets lined with false-front stores and a bustling boardwalk down both sides. The Good Lord never saw fit to put gold near Spearfish, but He did bless the area with fertile lands for farming and orchards. The town boomed with cattle and farming, in many cases with more stable wealth than other areas of the Hills.

Lula slowed her steps and he matched hers. "I've never actually been to town." Her sweet voice was a soft whisper then she shrieked and ducked her head. "It's Izzy and Harland Lawson from class! Hurry, before they see us!"

In the span of a heartbeat, he led her to the shadow of the covered boardwalk, protecting her from anyone seeing them from the opposite side of the road. He glanced over his shoulder and prayed no one had noticed them. The school only let in a select number of people, if students didn't follow the rules, others who would could be easily found. It would take only one report and both of them would be finished. And Harland Lawson was just the type of student who would report them, though, from the talk he'd heard on the other side of the room, there was a darker side to Harland's quiet.

Lula's hand fitted against Barton's arm as if it were made just to settle there. The curved muscle he'd earned from years of ranch work was easy for her to hold onto. Now that the danger of seeing Izzy had passed, she could almost enjoy herself. Being on the arm of a handsome man had never been a possibility, yet, here she was. Lula glanced back over her shoulder, just to make sure they'd left her friend, and potential discovery, far behind.

Barton directed her into a large livery and the smell of the barn, and home, assailed her. She'd helped clean the horse barn in Deadwood many times, and the smell was just the same. He led her to a stall with a large black horse. Everything about her was black, except for one white sock. She was a beautiful mare, even if the most visible part was the horse's rump. Star stomped and shifted, she was more spirited than anything Lula had ever ridden in the past. Good thing Star was not for her.

Barton leaned over her shoulder. "Don't worry. The one I had in mind for you is right over here." Star heard his voice and turned to find him. She had a long blaze down between her eyes almost to her muzzle. Star's eyes were soft as she notched her chin to get free of the halter holding her in the stall. Barton patted her flank softly. "Just a minute, girl. We'll get you out of jail in a flash."

The soft way he spoke to Star, like she was a cherished friend and not merely horseflesh, reminded her of the men back at the ranch. Her beloved brother in laws. Barton whisked her past the stalls of two other horses, then stopped by a sandy bay, with gentle brown eyes.

Barton rested his hand on her back as she observed the horse, excitement swirled around her, drowning her other senses. Barton whispered behind her. "She's a few years older, but still a good girl. The liveryman assured me yesterday that she was as gentle as the day is long and perfect as a mount for someone who might not ride much. I didn't know, so I wanted to be sure..."

Somehow, the idea that he'd been thinking about their time together made it more personal than she'd expected. He'd thought ahead to her comfort. Hadn't he warned her that his plan was to woo her right into his arms? Why hadn't she believed him? Her heart had been so hard she hadn't listened, and now she'd have to guard it or be in just the situation Izzy had warned about.

Barton disappeared to go find the liveryman, leaving her with her musings. Could she enjoy the remainder of the day knowing full-well his intentions? Even if she didn't succumb to feelings for him, because that was preposterous, was it right to lead him along; to spend time with him, when their new friendship could never go any further than it already had? He'd given her the option to keep running from him if she found him lacking. The old Barton was bound to show up at some point and steal this new joy. He always did. Barton always ruined everything, eventually, but did she trust herself not to become too attached before he did? It was already difficult to study with him around. Her sister, Ruby, had always said, *get too close to the stove, don't be surprised when you get burned*. Was she putting herself right on the stove?

Barton led her horse past her and out into the street. She was saddled and ready. Lula followed at a distance, then realized there was no fence or step for her to use to mount. She'd have to rely on Barton. He waited for her, anticipation plain on his face. He knew what she was thinking. A man who knew her thoughts could hurt her mightily, but she pushed that away and stepped forward. At the thought of his hands touching her, excitement welled inside her.

"Her name is Clover and she's all ready for you. I'll be out with Star in just a minute."

She started to nod, but before she could protest, his hands were on her waist and he'd turned her and lifted her into the saddle without even hitching his breath. His strong hands only lingered long enough to make sure she was steady in her seat before he was gone to get Star. Lula had never felt quite so light-headed. She arranged her legs properly in the side saddle horn as Barton led Star out of the livery and mounted. She'd almost schooled her breathing back to normal as he clicked twice to Star and led them out of town. Clover accepted gentle cues, which was good. Lula hated to use the riding crop as she followed Barton to the outside of town and down a narrow path.

Star pranced until the terrain was too steep, then she clipped along at a steady walk. Clover let Star act as the lead mare, perfectly content to remain quite a few paces behind. Even when Lula tried to encourage her to catch up so she could talk to

Barton, Clover quickly fell back to her old pace. Star's walking gate was just faster than Clover's. It gave Lula ample opportunity to watch Barton. At school, for two straight years, he'd been the head of the class, the one all the boys looked up to, both for his money and his antics. The teachers had loved him. Now, he was as steady on horseback as he was in every other situation. Calm, as if life had never thrown him anything he couldn't handle. Until her. He hadn't handled her well at all, still wasn't if he thought he could make her give up her dreams for him. She had too much at stake to let him convince her otherwise.

The trail veered deeper into the trees and then opened up slightly. There was an open area where the cropped grass and other leavings indicated they wouldn't be the first to leave their horses there. The ride had been pleasant, if short. She held her breath and tried to prepare for Barton's hands on her again as he dismounted and tied Star to a nearby tree. Her pulse sprinted to a frantic pace as he set his sights on her and swaggered toward her. That very same walk would've warned her in the past that she'd better be careful, some trickery was headed her way. Not now. Now, his swagger held a confidence that was alluring, even thrilling, not terrifying.

"You ready to come down from your tower, Rapunzel?" he waited by her left knee looking up at her as if she really were some fairytale princess. Or, did he have the same intent as the prince? To lure her with sweet words, have his way with her, then leave her to deal with the reality of life? She gasped and pulled away from him.

She laughed, suddenly nervous and unsure of herself. She leaned back in the saddle. Clover shifted under her and she gripped the reins, not sure if she really wanted to get down at all. It might be easier just to ride back down the hill than face the feelings dancing around inside her. He'd always made her nervous, why did it have to be so different now?

"Rapunzel? What foolishness." It was all she could think of to say before his hands were on her hips and she rushed to untangle her legs from the horn. Then she was on solid ground and his head was dipped slightly, looking down into her eyes. He had but to lean forward and she would be as lost as Rapunzel, but she wasn't as naive as the fairytale princess whose story was used to warn little girls to be virtuous, not foolish.

"Thank you for letting down your hair," his voice rumbled over her, his chin almost touching her forehead and she stepped back, unable to breathe. He was too close to her. Clover shied as Lula backed into her and Barton grabbed the reins and led her away. This day would be like riding in a hot air balloon—if Barton didn't keep back from her—filled with both awe and paralyzing fear. But no one could deny the beauty. She couldn't think of a woman alive who wouldn't think Barton was handsome, just as anyone who was lucky enough to ride in a balloon would surely see the wonder of God's creation and surely call it beautiful. But being that high, with the potential to fall...

Barton called to her from a small trail and she strode toward him. The trail was darker through the trees and he held out his hand to her. She'd wanted to resist holding his elbow earlier, but now, with no chance that anyone would see, and the uncertainty of the trail, she wouldn't hesitate. His strong hand locked around hers, leading her forward, and the path ahead became easier to see. If only the path for her life was just as clear.

Chapter Ten

Tree limbs brushed up against Barton's face and arms and he did his best to keep them from hitting Lula. She dodged around them well, used to the foliage in the hills. Would she relax near the falls, let him talk to her as he'd wanted from that first day? Would she listen to his idea and melt in his arms, or fight him and run? Lula had proven to have more fight in her than he'd thought, and he loved the spirited flicker in her eyes.

"How long did you say you've lived in Deadwood?" If he didn't make use of the time and actually talk to her, then he was more of a fool than he thought. She'd never open up to him if he didn't start slow, easy. Get to know even more about her than he'd been gaining by just paying attention for years.

"Almost six years. I live with my sister and brother-in-law, since my father is dead and my mother left our care to my sister."

How could a mother just give up on her daughters? He'd never leave Lula to anyone else. His mother hadn't ever abandoned her children, not even when Pa had told her what Barton had done to Lula. Instead, she'd hugged him close and admonished him to make it right, but didn't even turn her back on him, much less leave. "Was she ill or something?"

"No, but there was eight of us, counting Ruby, and she had no way to make enough money to support us. No home. Ruby had just married Beau and offered to take us. Ma was tired and found a good man that she helps back in Montana, but he didn't have enough to support all of us either. We still write to her often. She's been to a few of my sisters' weddings and is proud of me for attending Spearfish."

"Did you say, eight?" Four boys had been enough. His ma had wanted a daughter but had never been blessed with one. Now, her older sons were all ready to take over the ranch, but not a one of them was married. Ma still didn't have her daughter, not even by law. When he brought her home, she'd love on Lula.

"Yes, eight. There's Ruby, Jennie, Hattie, Eva, Frances, me, Nora, and Daisy. All except Nora, Daisy, and me are married. But that isn't my goal."

He stopped in front of her and turned to face her. She barreled right into him and he wrapped his arm around her to steady her from falling. He held tight to her elbow until she met his gaze. It wasn't her intention to fall, he knew that much. She *was* in teaching school, after all. But most women chose teaching because they needed the money, didn't have someone to care for them. Lula just didn't realize he was right there, waiting to give her everything the world had to offer.

"Don't your sisters have happy marriages?"

She tilted her head, her eyes narrowed in confusion. She could tell he was looking for something and was puzzling just what. She didn't back away from him for once and he reveled in her soft curves held tight against him.

"Yes, they do. But I want to be so much more than just a wife."

Just a wife... That she could never be. She would be the best wife. "Would you ever call your sisters 'just wives'?"

She tensed, seeing now where he was going with his line of questions.

Her jaw quivered over her words, "Well, no. Not to their faces for sure. I wouldn't want to dredge up the past."

The past? He was talking about her future, and his. "I'd bet they have happy and fulfilling lives." He couldn't stop from touching her, she was right there in his arms. He ran his hand up the back of her arm. A flash of fear in her eyes sliced him in two as she stepped back and took a deep breath.

"Was that your purpose today, Mr. Oleson? To talk me into giving up on teaching? I don't think you quite understand what it means to me."

He sighed and turned from her. She was slipping further from him, not physically, but even the use of his name was cold. "No. My purpose was to see the falls and to talk with you. Should we keep going or would you rather go back?" The stiffness in his own words rankled. Was he going to give up before fording the first river? Didn't he owe it to Lula to try harder? Didn't she deserve the privileged life as his wife and didn't he deserve the woman of his dreams?

He strode ahead and gave her a few minutes without his presence to think. Talking had been his goal, and he hadn't done much of it besides scaring her off.

"Barton, wait!"

He stopped and turned from his course as she looked up, they hadn't gone more than a few yards from the horses, he could still see them behind her. She was worth every moment, but would she allow herself to relax and let happen what he'd been feeling in his own heart for two years?

"I'm sorry." She pushed ahead to reach him. "You asked if I would ever call my sisters *just wives*? The answer is no. But they, also, have different lives and dreams. I've wanted to be a teacher for as long as I can remember. I want to spend time with you, Barton. But it must be as friends, please. Please don't ask me to give up my dream, don't tempt me away from it."

Could she have asked anything

more difficult of him? Lula stared up at him with those clear blue eyes, waiting on him for confirmation he didn't want to give, couldn't give, not unless he gave up his whole purpose for coming back, for going through class all summer. His whole intention had been to slowly draw her away from being a teacher and into his arms. He could teach if one of them must, and she could help him if she still wanted to, but she wouldn't need to do anything. Even the one forth share he'd get as the youngest would be plenty for them to live on for the rest of their lives.

He reached up and took one curl between his rough thumb and forefinger, rolling it softly. It silkiness too fine for his mind to ever recall exactly, and a fresh wonder every time. Could he give up on her, on everything he'd ever dreamed so that she could follow hers? Wasn't that what love was? He'd been so sure he loved her, but the idea of letting her go ripped a hole somewhere deep inside him.

"I won't tempt you away from anything. But might I still call you my friend? I find that being the teacher is much lonelier than I originally imagined." He let her lock of hair go and stepped back from her. Afraid of scaring her off further.

"I'm so sorry. I never imagined you as lonely." Her eyes softened and she drew closer; almost in his arms as she'd been before.

The muffled rush of the falls behind him was as good a distraction as any. As the assistant professor, he was too young to associate with Professor Cook and though he was the same age as everyone in his class, he was also forbidden from making friendships, his roommate had a whole separate life as a teacher and was almost ten years older. His life at home was a social one, with the hands, his brothers, or his parents always there, and the frequent celebrations they had. He didn't want her pity though, he wanted more and couldn't have it.

"Let's go take a look at those falls." He ducked under the nearby low branches and came out on the other side near the river. Mossy limestone walls towered above them, lending to the feeling of complete solitude. A man could get used to surrounding himself with God's creation, both the river and the woman called to his spirit more than he'd felt pulled in a long time. Lula stepped next to him and gasped, then came around him and held her hand out to feel the spray of the falls. "It's so beautiful."

It didn't hold a candle to Lula. The wonder in her eyes took his breath away. "I heard tell that a guy climbed up those falls like some Roman conqueror, then got stuck. Had to tiptoe his way back down or risk falling in front of his lady friend."

Lula chuckled next to him. "Who would do such a thing? That rock is wet and covered in moss. It must be dreadfully slippery."

"Oh, it is." He couldn't help but laugh at the story his closest friend from school had told him. He'd brought a girl to the falls with the intention of sneaking a sweet or two. He'd tried a little too hard to be a man and scared her half witless. She never gave him a kiss that day, but they were now engaged, so there had to be something to the show. "Want me to give it a go?"

A gasp escaped her lips, then a giggle that brought a smile to his own. "I do not! You'll get yourself killed. I don't want to have to ride all the way back alone to go for help."

He clutched his chest, more to hold in his laughter than his hurt.

"You wound me, Lula. I could handle myself over a few rocks."

"Yes, well, it wouldn't be a good way to end our outing. You can't exactly talk to me if they're carting you down the hill on a liter because you cracked open your skull."

Barton chuckled. "I'm sure I'd still manage to say more than I ought. I always have."

Her gaze rounded on him, soft but with purpose. "You told me you'd tell me why you pestered me so terribly." She turned and stared at the falls, her back a stark rod, not the welcoming relaxed curve of when they were joking. "I think I'm ready to know."

"*I* don't think you're ready to hear, and it doesn't matter now." And it didn't, not if she wanted to be a teacher more than she wanted him.

She huffed. "So you say. It didn't ruin two years of your life. Now, you talk to me, smile, yank me behind bushes as if my feelings don't matter a bit. I'm willing to forgive you, to be the friend you want me to be, but it starts with forgiveness. Give me a reason to forgive you."

She might give him grace for all his offenses of the past years, but would she ever forgive his biggest and most recent? The whole reason he'd come to school? None of the other stuff even mattered in light of that. If she truly wanted nothing to do with him, better that she think of him the way he was before. Better that she hate him than wonder what he'd been up to, that he'd prayed she would think more of him than her dream. She wanted everything; answers, truth, kindness, friendship, yet separation. What reason did he have to continue? Nothing, from what he could see.

A chipmunk skittered to the edge of the water a foot away from his boot. Friendly creatures. They'd been tamed by treats from people just as people had tamed the land. He glanced at Lula and narrowed his eyes, giving her the devilish grin she'd forced him to perfect over the last two years. "Truth is, jokes on you, Buttercup. I haven't changed a bit." He sprang on the chipmunk and grasped it tightly about the waist as it shrieked in protest, then rushed Lula. He dove to the ground lifting the hem of her skirt just a bit as he let the rodent go underneath, then ran down the short trail for his horse as Lula screeched at him to no avail.

Hot anger burned his chest the

whole way as he lost her screams to the sound of Star's hooves.

Chapter Eleven

Lula hopped around as she shrieked, lifting and swishing her skirts until the terrified creature ran back into the forest. It would be hard to say who was more frightened, the rodent, or her. One second she'd been sure she'd finally have answers about Barton that would help her move on, the next, he'd tossed that *thing* under her hems. And that look on his face...so like the boy he'd claimed he wasn't anymore.

The joke *was* on her. She'd believed him. He'd waltzed into the class on that first day with a debonair smile and a gentleman's attitude, and he'd convinced her his heart had changed. Even when her mind had told her to stop, to be cautious, she'd ignored it. Now he was gone. The sound of Star's hooves had long faded, the dust of the narrow track settled. She was good and stuck with Clover and no way to mount. There wasn't a fence she could climb or even a branch low enough to use. Drat saddles for women! Made so that they would be forever dependent on a man. Well, never again. She wouldn't trust Barton or anyone else. That had been her whole goal in becoming a teacher, to never need a man. Her father, not Beau but her real father, had claimed girls were worthless creatures. It was one of the few memories she carried of him. But it had stuck. She wasn't worthless. She'd prove him wrong. Lula Arnsby could take care of herself.

The reins had been tied in an infernally hard knot and she stood there for far longer than she wanted, trying to untie it. Didn't the man know it only needed to be looped if the horse was broke well? Of course, he did. He'd been planning even when they arrived to leave her up there.

Hadn't she learned anything after two years? Her hands shook with her anger, making the task all the more difficult.

A few drips fell from above, then more, and soon a downpour drenched her to the skin, leaving her white shirt clinging to her skin. She was suddenly thankful of all the other layers she wore. Clover didn't seem to be bothered in the slightest by the weather, but, without the sun, the late September air chilled her to the bone. Just as quickly as the downpour came, it abated, and though her hands shook and the reins slid through her fingers, she managed to get poor Clover untied.

"Well, girl. I guess we get to walk down the hill, not that you ever wanted to do much more than walk anyway. I can't get back up there on my own. I hope it isn't far. It felt like such a short ride up here." Would she make it back by supper time? If Barton showed his face in the cafeteria, she'd give him a piece of her mind. Loudly. Well, she could dream of such things, she'd never actually *do* it. Forcing a confrontation with him had never worked in the past and it wouldn't work in the future either. She'd be expelled for meeting him in private. He'd won yet again. Would always win. Because now he was the teacher's assistant and had power over her.

What could have possibly gone so wrong? She'd only asked him to tell her what he'd already promised to. They were both at Spearfish Normal to be teachers, so nothing else she'd said should've been a shock to him. Oh, how he'd played to her emotions! Telling her he was lonely! And her fool heart had fallen on his every word. Perhaps it would be better for her to transfer out of the school? Though, this was the closest to home, and the best in the area. Why should she give up just because of him? He'd been a beast, but she'd never given up before. She'd show him just how strong an Arnsby girl could be.

The trail was steeper than she remembered, and walking down in her half-boots was hard, especially with her heavy wet skirts twining around her legs. She slipped and tripped her way down, finally making it to the main road that led back into Spearfish. Would he be there at the livery, waiting to laugh at her? Her skirt was a filthy ruin from her muddy hems all the way up to the hand prints down her sides where she'd wiped them after a few falls. Her cheeks and face felt filthy and her hair hung in limp, damp tendrils around her face. The heat of shame burned up her cheeks. He'd embarrassed her for the last time.

A handsome young liveryman came running toward her. "Miss, miss! Are you all right? When Mr. Oleson came back alone, we worried." She handed him the reins and limped toward the bench in front of the livery. "I'm glad you made it back fine. I'll get Clover back in her stall, it'll be $1 for her rental."

He couldn't possibly be speaking to her. "He didn't pay for Clover?" She turned to look him in the eye and make sure she'd heard properly.

"No, miss. He said you were an independent woman who wanted to do for yourself and that you'd chafe at the collar if he paid for you." The boy's eyes were wide and he backed away from her like she might whip him with her riding crop, so she stood and handed it to him. He flinched, then took it from her.

"I don't have any means to pay for the ride. I was under the impression he was renting her for me. What can I do to earn the dollar for using her, at least for the ride *up* the hill?" It wouldn't be possible to wreck her clothes any more than they already were. At least she knew how to clean horse stalls.

"I wish I could just take it out of my pay, but honest, miss, I don't make that much."

Which meant that she wouldn't make that much, either. Now she was really in a bind. She had about forty cents sewn into the bottom hems of her skirts to keep them from swirling in a wind, but that wasn't all that much closer to a full dollar. "So, what could I do to earn about sixty cents?" She prayed he'd answer soon. Her wet stays were rubbing welts under her arms.

The boy ducked his head. "I'll ask the boss if you can muck out all the stalls for that. You sure you got the rest?"

No, she wasn't. It wasn't as if she put the same coins in every skirt. She'd only used whatever was available at the time. "I'm fairly certain. If you'd be so kind as to ask your boss?" She sat on the bench again, wiping her arm over her forehead. The grime on her arm made her groan. She crossed her leg over her knee to get at her hems. Did it matter now if she was ladylike? She was about to get up to her ankles in horse mess. The hem tore easily and she collected the coins within, counting each one as she came to the little pocket she'd sewn for each. There was more than she'd thought, with ten nickels stored evenly spaced around her skirt.

As she stood, the overly long fabric now dragged on the ground. An older man approached her with a pipe hanging limply out the side of his mouth. "You the lady who can't pay?"

No, she was the lady left to pay a bill she hadn't realized she'd have. "I have half. What can I do to earn the rest?"

"Nothing. I won't have no woman in here fouling up the place. Next thing you know, there'll be rumors that I'm hiring woman-folk to care for my horses." He shoved his hand in front of her. "I'll take what you got, then git."

Anger built in waves, starting in her head and flowing right down to her shaking hands. She'd get Barton Oleson, and he'd regret ever speaking to her.

Barton raked his hands through his hair. He'd let his anger get the better of him. It didn't take deep thoughts to picture his ma's disapproving eyes if she knew what he'd done. All the things he'd done. From touching her skirt to putting that poor critter where he had. Then leaving her behind. And the foulest thing of all, making her pay for her horse. At least he'd been too focused on the chipmunk to pay attention to anything *under* those skirts. He clenched his fist. His pa would call him worse than a road apple and dirtier than the belly of a snake. He felt it all the way down to the toes of his boots. If only he could get what he felt under control, but he'd never been good at that where Lula Arnsby was concerned.

Oh, she'd be thinking about him tonight all right, thinking about how best to turn him in and send him home. Hadn't he told her he'd accept the full blame if she did? If any other man had attempted to do to her what he'd just done, he'd pound them just for thinking about it. He flexed his hands and shook the tension away. The school was just ahead. He'd write her a note telling her he was sorry for his behavior, then he'd talk to professor Cook and withdraw as his assistant. It was obvious he couldn't be trusted with Lula. Good thing he'd realized it so quickly, before he'd pulled them deeper into something neither of them would've been happy in. How could she ever trust him when he couldn't be trusted?

Frank rushed toward him, his face frantic. "Where have you been? Cook fell off a ladder while painting his house. He won't be able to teach for weeks. So, you've got one weekend to get over there and prepare for the rest of the year. Congratulations, you've just been hired as the new teaching professor!"

Chapter Twelve

Two days later, Barton stood in front of the empty classroom trying to remember every point of the lecture Cook had given him for that day. He did his best to memorize it the rest of Saturday and after the church service on Sunday. There had been no rest on *his* Sabbath. Even now, he wanted to resort to the notes he'd written. He'd also have to do all the duties of an assistant, since now he didn't have one. His morning had been full of cranking the mimeo and rushing about making sure the room was prepared.

He'd never gotten around to writing that note to Lula and now he'd be required to stand in front of her for a whole day, forcing himself to not stare at her. Reminding himself what he had to do, which was anything but talk to her. She didn't want him to. Hadn't really wanted him ever.

His showing her the kind of man he was now should've made her want to live her life with him. But she kept pushing him away. Why had she even agreed to come riding if she didn't want to actually spend time with him? He'd been crazy enough to think that she could ever forgive him or that one year of good could make up for two years of bad. And, he hadn't even made it through a full month without proving her right. He hadn't changed a bit. His bad decisions still ruled him.

The swift scent of rose petals washed over him and a muffled gasp told him without turning around that Lula had made it into the room. Early, like she usually was. Briefly, he wondered how she'd explained her late return to Izzy. Just as he'd made it back to Spearfish, it had rained. Had she gotten soaked in the downpour? That would prove even harder to explain. What had that agile mind of hers come up with to cover for being with him, or had she told Izzy all?

Izzy would be with Lula, they rarely went anywhere alone. Muffled whispers proved his theory correct, but the prickles up his arms also told him that Lula was staring at him, making it difficult to concentrate on the points he was writing. He finished the few notes on the board and turned. Izzy smiled at him and Lula pegged him with a glare fit to light him ablaze. If only he hadn't been an idiot and could channel that fire.

"Good morning, ladies." He put on his professional voice, cold, distant. "Professor Cook has taken a bad turn, so you'll have to put up with me as your professor for the remainder of the year."

Izzy clicked her tongue and shook her head. "Yes, we heard. Poor man. Something about falling off a ladder."

Lula fixed those deep blue eyes on him. "Did you sway his ladder so you'd get his job?"

Her barbed words hit the mark. She *would* think so little of him. Unfortunately, he couldn't reply in kind, not knowing how much she'd told Izzy. Izzy's suddenly ruddy cheeks and wide eyes said Lula hadn't told her anything and she was now mortified for her friend. Though Lula obviously wasn't, her eyes popped in defiance. Sweet mercy, she was beautiful when she was angry.

"Lula Matilda Arnsby! What a horrible thing to say!" Izzy huffed.

Lula *Matilda*? He couldn't hide his smirk. Good thing he wasn't the only one whose parents had poor taste in a middle name.

But he'd get her for her words. Make her think about him all evening long. Maybe he'd also load all the students up with just a little more work, as well. "Yes, Miss Arnsby, it was a horrible thing to say. As punishment, I think we need to go back to primer school basics. You will write, *I will not say rude or nasty things to Mr. Barton Oleson ever again, as long as I shall live.*"

Lula sat back in her chair and her eyes burned with anger at him.

"One hundred times, Miss Arnsby. Due tomorrow at the head of class. Oh, and please move to the front. I don't want you in the back where you can get yourself into trouble. I suddenly feel the need to keep an eye on you."

"Why...you!" She growled.

He tapped the front seat that he'd occupied the first day. In the front row, right next to where he'd be teaching. At least he couldn't stare at her, she'd be too close. If Lula was going to hate him the rest of her life, at least he'd give her a reason.

Lula couldn't bear to sit in the front for another day. She could feel the eyes of every student on her, wondering just what she'd done. When he'd publicly asked her to hand in her sentences four days ago, she'd been mortified. Worse, he'd taken the papers and looked them over, finally smiling down at her, his gaze far too warm for her comfort.

In the last few days, she'd found herself wishing that she could have the Barton from the first few weeks of school back. He'd pestered her, and got her to thinking about hope and what it meant to forgive. If it had been his mission to teach her what it was like to be cursed and without forgiveness, this week had done it. She'd paid the penalty, writing the awful lines until her hands cramped, stalling over his name by the end. But, he had yet to let her return to her seat near the back by Izzy and he wouldn't let Izzy sit near her in the front, for fear she would make trouble. She remained in punishment well after what he'd originally set.

Though the primary school teachers they'd had would agree with his assessment that she was trouble, she wasn't. Had never sought to be a nuisance. If the current slide of her grades said anything, Barton wasn't feeling especially friendly to her in the evening as he was grading for the day either. Though she'd also noticed he'd piled them with work, far more than Cook had been. How he managed to be ready for lecture every day, after grading all of their work at night, was amazing. Even if she didn't like to admit it. If she had to apologize for her rash words to get to sit back by Izzy and reduce the workload, she would. Perhaps then she could at least get away from him. He tended to linger close to her as he was lecturing, even resting his hip against her desk. Far too close to her. Why wouldn't her heart go back to hating him after what he'd done? Why did it trip and hope for a glance from him even after he'd admitted his words from the first two weeks were a lie?

The last few minutes of class ebbed by and Barton dismissed

everyone. His gaze lingered on her for one moment longer than anyone else and heat traveled to her belly. Izzy approached her and laid a hand on her shoulder.

"Are you ready, Lula? Harland has invited me to have ice cream again. His friend isn't with Molly anymore and he was wondering if you wanted to go with us? So it isn't uncomfortable, of course."

Barton stiffened at the blackboard as he wiped it clean. Would it bother him if she agreed to go? Somewhere inside, whether he was ready to admit it or not, he wanted her to give up on her dreams...probably for him. The thought was terrifying. She'd waited so long, tried so hard to get where she was. Going to the Normal School for the last two years of her education had been the only way to make sure she got into the teaching school. She'd begged Beau and Ruby to let her go. They hadn't wanted to, but she'd promised to work as hard as she possibly could. She'd kept up every single grade, no matter how difficult, to get right where she was. How could he ever ask her to give that up?

Harland's friend wasn't handsome in the slightest, and she didn't want to go. His nose ran constantly, forcing him to wipe it and snuffle in a most unbecoming manner. It was far from attractive. His laugh was loud, filling a room, causing everyone nearby to stare. She'd been one to do it, and she didn't need him forming an attachment to her in any way.

Lula bit her lip to give herself a moment to think. "I'll catch up with you in a minute." Izzy pursed her lips and nodded, glancing to Barton at the board, then left them alone.

Barton's movements picked up speed, became choppy, as if he was suddenly in a rush. Maybe he aimed to get away from her quickly. "I thought I'd warned you before about dawdling in my classroom, Miss Arnsby." He didn't even turn to speak to her, yet he knew she was there. He'd known they were alone, or he never would've spoken. The role of teacher changed him, or maybe she'd just been fooled from the start of the year, seeing only what she wanted to. Didn't everyone wish for their tormentor to have a change of heart?

"Yes, you did. But you were much more kind about it before. Perhaps the status of professor has gone to your head?" Oh, why couldn't she keep her mouth shut? It was an awful

Arnsby trait. None of her sisters were able to hold their tongue. Except Daisy, she was silent, like Beau. She'd learned from him growing up, that the best way to figure out a problem was to listen instead of talk. Lula should've taken that advice.

"I'm sorry, Mr. Oleson. That was uncalled for." She dipped her head slightly as he turned to look at her.

"I should say so. Wouldn't want to have you do more lines. I would think the first hundred times would've been enough."

She sucked in her pride. It had been so difficult to write his name, but probably not for the reasons he thought. She'd formed an attachment as she'd written those lines. "They were. I wanted to say that I'm sorry for saying such spiteful words to you on Monday. I was still hurting from the weekend, but I shouldn't have said anything and certainly not in front of Izzy. I've learned my lesson."

He nodded then turned back to his work of clearing the board.

"Does that mean I'm forgiven and can go back to sitting in the back with Izzy?"

He whipped around and leveled her with ice blue eyes. "It isn't my job to forgive you, Lula. It's my job to teach you. That's what you've left me with, and not one jot more. I'll make the best teacher out of you that I'm able, since that's all you want from me."

He slammed a dollar down on the desk and collected his books as he strode for the door. "Good day, Miss Arnsby."

Chapter Thirteen

The crumpled dollar bill from Barton's pocket lay curled on her desk. He'd been ready to give it to her. It hadn't been in a money clip or wallet, just sitting there, bunched at the ready to give her. Had he known that she would apologize and he'd throw that day right back at her? Reminding her again why she shouldn't want what she couldn't have. But didn't everyone? And why *did* she? He'd been so horrible to her the entirety of the time she'd known him. Yet, the very same thoughts were now turned on their head. What had occupied her every waking moment before in avoiding him, now took up equal residence in finding him.

Izzy had said as much before her outing with Harland, and now she was going again. She'd fallen into the same trouble she'd been worried about. Lula had been warned and had discounted it. She'd looked forward to the outing with Barton so much that she'd put him on a pedestal he couldn't possibly have wanted.

She sighed and collected the crumpled bill, tucking it into her book. It would replace the skirt she'd had to throw away, but even that didn't make her feel better. A skirt was one thing. Barton's hurt was another. Just as she'd always been able to tell when he was about to pull a stunt on her in the past, she could now tell he was angry, not honest. He'd never switched his mood when he'd gone after her before. She'd been his sole target then, and she was growing to suspect she was still, in a wholly different way.

If she'd hurt him, made him angry, then she could fix it. He could go back to being the Barton that teased her with soft crinkles near his eyes, not the one with pithy retorts and something that flared between anger and need in his eyes.

Her books would keep on her desk for a minute. Barton couldn't leave the building until he'd locked up the room, so he couldn't be far. A quick glance down the hallway to see if anyone lingered and she turned left, deeper into the building, to where she'd heard the teachers had a small room for preparation at the end of the hall. If any other teachers were in there, she'd leave. But, if she found him alone...

The thought stopped her in the middle of the narrow hall. What would she do? Beg him to tell her what had caused his angst? He hadn't been willing to tell her anything last Saturday. He'd turned back into his old self after she'd asked him, though. So, perhaps he just didn't wish to bring it up further. If she really wanted to give him forgiveness, and he asked it of her, did it really matter why he did all those things from their past? Could he change them? Would knowing fix the damage he had done? He'd said he never meant to hurt her, wasn't that enough? Or, was that just another lie?

Her steps echoed off the walls, but she could hear nothing else. If there was a room for teachers, they didn't use it to talk. She slowed her steps and held her breath. Peeking into a private room was rude and sneaky. She softly cleared her throat. "Mr. Oleson?" Her words, though soft, vibrated in her ears in the cavernous hall with its high ceilings.

Barton's voice came from within the room. Quiet, almost defeated. "Why did you follow me, Lula?"

He wouldn't call her that if there were any chance that someone else would hear. She calmed her racing heart and took a deep breath as she forced her steps into the room. "We need to talk, Mr. Oleson." No, that wasn't right. He just couldn't be Mr.

Oleson to her. He was beginning to mean too much. "Barton, please."

He sat on a chair, his head hung low between his shoulders and resting in his hands. He raised his head just enough to look at her. "We've already established that there's nothing to say and that being alone together is a *very* bad idea. I think you should turn around and leave, right now."

If it was such a bad thing, why did it feel so right to try to bring him around, even if it meant being alone with him for just a few minutes. "Barton. I don't care what you said. I'm choosing to ignore it. I don't care why you did what you did in years past. I forgive you. You were a new man the beginning of this year, a man...that I find I miss. Would you please accept my apology? So that we can be back on friendly terms."

Apologies were so hard. She'd been forced into so many with this man. All those from the past had been cold and usually followed by a mental curse of his very name, but not now. She *wanted* his forgiveness, wanted him to stop hurting. He stood so quickly she jumped back. His long strides made quick work of the space between them and she held her breath as he stood before her with flashing eyes and broad shoulders. His gaze penetrated her very soul and she could hide nothing from him.

"You ask a lot of me, Lula. I want so much for you..." He stopped and rested his forehead against hers, the nearness of him, so very close she could wrap her arms around him. How could she need that? But it was a need, one she had to fight against. "You can't possibly know all the things I want for you. But if I can't have those things... It's better that you hate me. It's better that you leave this room right now and never turn around. Never talk of us or friendship again."

His words ignited a flame in her soul. She didn't want to turn or run. Nearness, not distance, was her craving. That wasn't who she was. She may have been flighty as a child, but never a quitter. "I must know what you want of me. I can't leave you like this, broken, knowing it's my fault. You say you never changed, but it's not true. This...person...you've been this week isn't the boy from a year ago. He's a brute, lording his title of teacher over all of us, but that wasn't how you were before. You haven't been yourself this last week and I can safely say I know the difference now. Every one of your students noticed."

Dare she reach out and touch him? His chest was right there, and he hadn't moved. His eyes were so close to hers they would be sharing a kiss if he but tilted his head. And the strangest of all, she wanted it. Her thoughts wouldn't mind her and despite their history, she wanted to share that intimacy with this man.

"You think I'm a brute?" He began to pull away and she reached up, holding the lapel of his coat so that he would not leave, not when he was so near. If he stepped away, he might never come back.

"No. I think you've been *acting* a brute. I think you're hurt and I think I hurt you. I'm sorry. I was trying to protect myself and in the process, I shoved you away. I'm so sorry."

He reached up and trailed his hand gently along her jaw sending a nervous tingle down her spine, but it wasn't enough. Was this how it all started? Was this how all her sisters had felt as they lost themselves to their men? His hand lingered for a moment and he groaned as he pulled her closer, crushing her for a moment in a fierce embrace. His lips came down upon hers. She clutched tighter to him as everything in creation but him disappeared for a moment. Surely the floor under her had vanished, for she was lighter than air.

His whole form went rigid and he pulled away from her. "I'm so sorry, Lula. I've wanted you for so long..."

Wanted her? She straightened her shirtwaist and made sure her skirts were still in order. "It's only been a few weeks since the start of school, Barton. I didn't expect a fire like that could be built so quickly."

He laughed humorlessly and faced the large sunny window, his form in glorious relief against it. "I'm sure you would think it's only been since the start of term, but no. I've loved everything about you since you arrived in my class with your impish little grin and your beautiful fairy hair. And now you know why I've been such a brute. A man gets surly when he wants what he'll never have."

To have and to hold, to have and to hold... Hadn't that been a line in each of the weddings she'd attended in the last five years. He wanted to have her. The memory of the heat of his arms around her, holding her, his lips pressed to hers.

Without her, he wasn't himself. It was a weighty and heady thought all at once. Were her goals more important than Barton? A mere month ago, the answer would have been 'no'. She pressed the butterflies in her belly into submission as she walked back to the classroom for her books. She hadn't run, but after he'd kissed her into distraction, and told her he wanted her for always, he'd told her to go. That he accepted her apology and that he would try to be back to himself. Even now, her body rebelled. Her feet wanted to turn and rush right back to him and hold onto him until he told all his secrets. Until she figured out this sudden ache inside her.

While she hadn't learned anything about his past, she had learned there was power in her touch. He might want her, but with a glance, a word, he'd give her the world. All she had to do was give up everything *she'd* ever wanted. Was it worth it? Could she give up every dream for Barton? She wasn't just here for herself, she was the first Arnsby to ever try to get an education. Wouldn't they be disappointed in her?

Her books lay in the classroom where she'd left them, the board still a cloudy mess from Barton's rushed exit. It would take but a minute to put it to rights and then he wouldn't have to do it before he locked up. Because he was the only teacher, there was a long list of chores on his shoulders. She collected the rag and cleaning alcohol from under the desk and set to work. The smell was horrid, but the board soon gleamed black, ready for tomorrow.

It might be too difficult to give up every notion she'd ever harbored about rescuing her own family's past, but she could help him in whatever way possible, spend free moments with him when she could, and pray he understood after graduation. She'd grown tough over the last two years, she would mend even if she did become attached to him. He could have her, for a time.

Izzy swung into the doorway. "There you are! I've been waiting two forevers for you! Did you forget all about the ice cream? We have to leave right now or we won't make it back in time for studying."

A purely wicked thought took root before she could pluck it out. "I'm sorry, Izzy. Mr. Oleson assigned me more lines to do after you left. I guess it's just too hard to keep my mouth shut. I was to start by cleaning the board for him." She held up the rag as proof, even though it wasn't true.

Izzy's eyes widened. "Why, Lula. Last time, you barely finished your lines and your homework. I think it's just horrid that he would do that to you. He's been so different since he took over teaching. Maybe he just doesn't recall all the work we need to do. He doesn't have half the studies we have." She stomped her foot and scowled. "I have half a mind to stomp right down to the cafeteria and give him wherefore."

Poor Barton wouldn't know what hit him. It would never do for Izzy to confront him since the lines weren't real. "You wouldn't! And risk him giving me more? You just go and have your fun. I'll be in the dorm when you get back."

A weak smile blushed across Izzy's lips. "It won't be near as fun without you. Harland is wonderful, but he tries so hard to include Amos that he forgets about me."

"I thought you didn't want to get too attached, that sounds like you're well on your way."

The edge of Izzy's lip tipped slightly. "He showed me an article from a school in the East where they are allowing married teachers to continue working. It's just a test, mind you. And not everyone is happy about it, and certainly not everyone is embracing it, but it's progress. And he says that if we do get close, he would try for such a position."

If there was one school trying it, there may be others. That would mean she and Barton wouldn't have to separate at the end of the term. "They are trying this? Where?"

Izzy shook her head. "I don't remember. It's only one school, far as I can tell. We'll be old and gray before they adjust the rules here."

But if they moved there...she might be able to have Barton and her dream, too. It was just a matter of convincing him he needed *her* more than he needed to stay in South Dakota. Didn't many teachers move to where the jobs were? He was a good teacher, that was evident. Even with his changed demeanor, he held the attention of a class of students whom he was equal in age to. He was meant to teach. Perhaps even more than she, and she'd dreamed of teaching for years. She wiped her hands on the rag and picked up her books. "That may be, but you're right, it gives me hope."

Lula rushed to her room and closed the door behind her. She had work to do, now more than ever. While she'd never been intentionally unruly. It was time to take a page from Barton's past in order to spend a little time with the teacher. But she had to do it in such a way that none of the other students saw her do it. Tarnishing her good standing would ruin everything. They would only take the most exceptional women teachers for that experimental teacher test, and they would have to be married. There was that tingle in her belly, like when he kissed her, all over again. She'd never find herself married if she didn't find a way to spend time with Barton.

She yanked out a blank sheet of paper and a pencil from her case, tapping it against her lip. He'd done many things to her in the past, giving her a bevy of options. "I'm so sorry, Barton. I hope you understand." She smiled as the list of what she had to do flowed down the paper and onto the back.

"Now, to pay a little penance even before I begin." She drew another blank sheet of paper from her notebook. *I, Lula Arnsby, will not put chewing gum on Mr. Barton Oleson's chair nor under his desk.* The sentence fit nicely across one line. Halfway down the sheet, where she was sure he wouldn't bother to look, she hesitated, then wrote, *I, Lula Oleson...*, just to see what it would look like. The look of it gave her pause. Her own sisters' new names sounded strange to her ears, but Lula Oleson sounded good, like she'd been born to have the name. Would he notice? She folded the sheet and bit her lip as a flight of giddiness came over her. Tomorrow morning, she'd need to get some gum.

Chapter Fourteen

The board had been cleaned when he'd come back to lock the room the day before. He'd waited until Lula had turned the corner in the hallway, afraid to be alone with her again so soon after he'd done the unthinkable; he'd let his guard down and pulled her in for a kiss that he couldn't keep from slipping into his thoughts. It had taken so long for her soft footfalls to leave the classroom, he'd been tormented with visions of her lips and soft sigh as she parted from him. She was too tempting to resist.

Two long years he'd waited to kiss her, but instead of slaking his cravings for Lula, they had intensified. Then, he'd rushed to the class to lock it up, just to realize that she'd cleaned up for him. Her thoughtfulness after he'd been a randy buffoon only sealed her as the perfect one for him. She could see through his surly bluster to who he was beneath and still cared enough to help him. Wasn't that what a good wife was called to do? Heat rushed over him once again. He wanted her for his wife more than anything he'd ever wanted.

But he couldn't be as bold anymore. If having her certificate meant that she had accomplished something, he could accommodate that, even embrace it—since it meant she would be right here with him in his classroom. Every day he could watch her grow and get closer to him. Then, on graduation day, he could ask her brother-in-law for her hand. She could graduate and begin plans for their wedding, all on the same day.

The next morning, at five minutes to the hour, Lula still hadn't arrived for class. She was usually early. Most of the other students, including her closest friend, Izzy, were already there. Was she afraid to see him after yesterday? Had thoughts of their kiss kept her awake all night as they had for him?

Two more minutes ticked by and Lula rushed into the classroom, a beautiful flush to her cheeks. She hit him with a conspiratorial grin and slowed her steps, stopping opposite of his desk in the front. All eyes were on her as she pulled a sheet of paper from her notebook.

She caught his glance and held it, her eyes possessed a wicked glint that left him unsure. What was she up to, and would anyone else notice her strange behavior? A quick glance at the men, all sitting on the left side of the room, and his suspicions were confirmed. Raised eyebrows and winks from the men made him want to groan aloud.

"Just as you *asked*, Mr. Oleson." She laid the paper down on his desk, turned and sat in her usual seat in the front.

Hadn't she sought him out yesterday just so she could have her way and return to sitting in the back? Had he been completely confused? And when did he assign her lines? Surely, that kiss hadn't left him so addle-pated he'd forget something like that? He scanned the paper, his eye immediately drawn to her mistake with her name. *I, Lula Oleson...* A lump lodged in his throat and he swallowed it swiftly. He had to get the class in order before anyone could notice anything further amiss. Lula couldn't get expelled. If she left, he'd have to leave too, which meant his fate was sealed at a ranch in Belle Fourche, not with a lovely teacher with soft lips and bouncy hair.

"Thank you, Miss Arnsby." He glanced up to see her popping a piece of gum in her mouth. She'd called it the devil's tool when he'd stuck a wad of it to her chair and it had gotten horribly meshed into the back of her skirt. Why would she chew it now, it was forbidden in the classroom, but should he make even more of a spectacle of her? If he did, the other students might notice his constant attention on her.

Something was amiss with his Lula and now he couldn't remember what he was supposed to be teaching about. His notes were stuffed in the back of his text book, if he'd put them in there that morning, with as muddled as his mind was. He flipped it open to regain his thoughts.

Sparks in Spearfish

The class seemed to drag by. Every time he turned to look at his notes, his glance would catch and hold on two words, *Lula Oleson*. Had she done that on purpose? After losing his place, he glanced up at her. She smiled at him with what could only be called a devilish grin. Was that the look he'd given her for the last two years? What was she up to and how could he stop it without bringing her undue attention?

Before he could control his own tongue, the words slipped free. "Miss Arnsby?" What had he been talking about? Every point of his notes had fled. "Can you come to the board and write down the four points from lecture today?" Letting her puzzle through it would give him a moment to figure out how to finish out the class time. He had a full hour yet and he'd bumbled through enough of the day.

As she came forward, he stepped back out of her way, handing her his chalk and letting his hand brush her palm. She smiled once then turned from him to go to a clean section of board. She calmly wrote the first two points, then her chalk scraped across the board with a deafening screech. It ground against his teeth and he turned away from her. When he turned back, she glanced at him. She had that grin in place that made him wary. Then she finished her two lines and placed the chalk in his hands, brushing the tips of her fingers down his palm as she strode by. The little cat was playing with him.

"Careful," she whispered. Almost too quiet for him to hear. What had she meant by that? He approached her answers and nodded. Giving too much praise might arouse suspicion, so he wouldn't do it, but she *had* gotten everything right.

He pulled out his seat and sat down, just as Lula gasped loudly. The ball of hard gum lay under his right thigh, he could feel it pressing into him. She had to have done it when she'd distracted everyone with the blackboard. He wanted to get up and yank her from her seat, pull her out in the hallway and make her fess up to whatever she was doing. She wasn't the sort to play games.

"Class is dismissed. Miss Arnsby, will you stay behind for a moment, please?"

Astonishingly enough, she looked pleased. There were a few more raised eyebrows and conspiratorial looks as the other students gathered their books and left. He and Lula couldn't get caught, and Lula's behavior and his own had pushed the boundaries.

She stood from her desk, her gaze not quite meeting his. Her hands wove behind her back as she approached his desk.

He waited until every last student was gone. She shifted uncomfortably in front of him, waiting for him to dole out some punishment, which was the farthest thing from his mind. When he was sure they were alone, he finally trusted his voice.

"This isn't like you, Lula. You're playing with fire. The students noticed your change in behavior. Are you trying to get caught so that you're sent home? Because I can't prevent that. If we're reported, we are both finished."

Her deep blue eyes finally looked up and widened. "No, not that. I didn't want anyone else to even notice." She held up her wrist with an intricate metal bracelet. "I scraped it across the board to make the noise, so no one would see...what I did to your chair." Her lips fluttered as she held back a giggle. "I warned you. I didn't think you'd actually sit back down."

"You warned me? That quiet 'be careful' with that little grin of yours? Is this how you felt when I used to play tricks on you?"

The side of her lip quirked up in playful smile. She was having far too much fun with her mischief. "Maybe."

"You've left me in a rather embarrassing position. At least when I put gum on *your* seat, you could hide it in the folds of your skirt. I don't have half enough fabric for that."

"You only just sat down. If you hurry, it might come loose quickly."

Her giggles took the edge off what little anger he could muster.

He stood and made a dash for her around the desk. Lula shrieked and danced to the other side, keeping the large teacher desk between them. He pulled the gum from his seat and tossed it in the trash, hoping it didn't leave a visible mark on the back of his leg. But he still wanted to catch her, wrap the little imp in his arms, quell the mischief, and replace it with fire. The fire he'd seen yesterday after his kiss.

If he gave up, she might stop running long enough for him to catch her. "Fine, you win." He held up his hands. "Just please, no more games in the class. I don't want to have to defend you to the president. It wouldn't look good. And if you have to stay after class too often, it will only be a matter of time before some curious student waits by the door to see what we're up to."

Their fun would have to come to an end. The school grounds were just too full of people who would be happy to turn them in.

"I'll clean the board for you." Lula came around his desk, done with playing for now.

He caught her wrist as she reached for the cleaning rag and it took all his will not to pull her into his arms. "You can help me if you wish, but I mean it, Lula. Behave. Don't try to do to me what I did to you." He lifted her wrist to his face, gently pressing his lips to the pulse point where it raced, then let her wrist loose and touched her cheek. Her breath hitched, and she covered his hand with hers. He hardly trusted his own voice. "I can see what you're trying to do, but it won't work."

She closed her eyes and nodded but he couldn't find the strength to let her go. "My weekends are so full now with learning the lectures... I don't know when I can see you again."

A smile flitted over her lips. "If it was meant to be, it will happen."

Oh, to have her faith.

Lula ripped her list into small pieces. While Barton had enjoyed her little game, he was right. Too much of that and the class would wonder just what she was doing. They wouldn't blame him, they would see it as her misbehavior, and she couldn't be sent home. They'd only been in school a little over one month, there was almost seven more to go. How could she sit through each day wanting to talk to only him, yet never see him? Had her heart changed so drastically in only a month?

Izzy strode in and, before she even closed the door, hitched her hands to her hips and glared down at her. "Lula Arnsby, you tell me what's going on this moment. You have never in your life acted so silly as you did today in class. Even Harland noticed and asked me if you were trying to get expelled."

Defending herself came much easier with Izzy, who knew her better than anyone. "And this coming from the same man who's trying to take you about town based on one news article? If you two fall in love, there is no hope. It's one school. Women who gave up teaching to marry from all over will flock to that one school for a chance." She would know, she'd be one of them. "I'm not trying to do anything. I'll tamp my behavior down, but Mr. Oleson needed to be reminded that occasionally students don't do just as you ask." But that hadn't been why she'd done it. And if he hadn't asked her to stop, she would've kept going. Just being with him was as addicting as the moonshine her father used to brew.

Izzy closed the door with a secure thud and her frown penetrated down to the hems of Lula's skirts. Every bit of her was heavy with anger. "If Harland and I ever go beyond friendship, which we haven't, he could still teach. I would be a homemaker, but we could still talk about his day and I would have an understanding, because I will know. I've been through this. If you keep this up, you can't just marry and move on. He's the teacher, Lula. You'll be expelled, and he could get fired. That is no way to start a future. If you think you have any feelings for him at all, stay away from him. Let him have his job. If you leave, he can still teach, and if he feels anything for you, he can court you next summer after graduation."

That wasn't anything like what she wanted. Her visions of standing in front of a group of perfect students, writing arithmetic problems on their little boards, while sitting at adjoined desks were fading fast. Maybe she was never meant to do such a thing. Her sisters had all said teaching would be hard, and that she was too much like a butterfly to ever be a good teacher. Too sweet, too bubbly, and unable to sit still long enough to get children to do the same.

"I don't know what I feel, Izzy."

"What you do is just the same, no matter what you feel. You leave him alone."

It was exactly the last thing her heart wanted to do. Even now, just minutes after his warm hand and devilish mouth had scorched her wrist with his touch, she craved more. She craved the things only a wife ever dared desire. Barton's frustration was so potent and so true.

Sparks in **Spearfish**

Even a woman could get surly when she wanted what she couldn't have.

"You'd best make your decision. Harland will follow the rules. If he catches you... Well, it would be better if you left before then. So, make your choice, but understand that whatever you choose carries consequences for others."

She knew it better than even Izzy. What right did she have to destroy Barton's livelihood? He'd done a full year of courses during one summer. He was driven and he'd make an excellent teacher. The other students had always loved him and, as their teacher, they would love him more. He was direct, honest, fun, and so much more. In seven months, she'd still have a year of student teaching to complete before she could teach. He'd be ready to start somewhere, probably far away. They would never end up teaching near each other and that was better, because the more time she spent with him, the more he took over all of her thoughts.

A knock came softly on the door and Izzy turned to answer. A small girl stood in the doorway with a sweet smile and a peppermint stick. She reached out a slip of paper and curtsied as she slipped the paper in Izzy's hand, then ran. Izzy looked at the small sheet of folded paper and frowned.

"Looks like he's making you choose right now." She handed over the paper.

Lula glanced at the note with her name on it. After he'd graded so much of her homework, his handwriting was now familiar to her. Reading it in front of Izzy would give away too much, but asking her to leave would be an admission that she wanted privacy.

"Are you so frightened to read it in front of me? What if he wants to meet you, right now? What if he wants to discuss your behavior from class, or worse, what if you've been reported already and he wants you to leave?"

All those things were possible and her stomach clenched with each one. They'd kissed in what she'd thought had been a private room, but could anyone have caught them? The hallway had echoed loudly, but she'd been so intent on Barton, would she have heard if someone had sneaked up on them?

It was possible, and her mischievous display today was right in front of the whole class. While she'd tried to be discreet, she'd failed miserably in attempting to do what had come so naturally to Barton. She flipped open the note. The message was brief.

Bush. 9PM. B

If anyone else had gotten their hands on that note, it would've meant nothing. There were many bushes all over campus and many people whose name started with B. But between her and Barton, there could only be one bush that he would talk about. The one on the edge of the administration building where they'd hidden to discuss going riding. Would he want to go again? He'd said he had no time, but she'd help him with his notes if it meant she could be with him.

"It's nothing. Not urgent. Don't concern yourself."

Izzy eyed her and sat slowly in the chair at the end of her bed. "You aren't going to meet him, are you?"

How could she have known? "It's nothing, Izzy. You need not worry about it."

"I do worry! You're my closest, most dear friend, and I see you throwing away what you've dreamed of for years because of a boy that you somehow think you can fix now. That's all this infatuation is. You think that now that he's nice to you, you can reform him. We women can't help but search for a problem we can correct, and Barton Oleson has been your biggest problem. Probably of your whole life. He will never love you, Lula. You can't change that much. He likes the attention from you now, and he'll take it as far as he can go, then you'll drown in your sorrow when you find out he's just the same as he always was."

"It's not that way, Izzy. He really has changed. He claims..." No, she couldn't tell Izzy that he'd wanted her from the moment he'd first seen her. She'd never believe it even though Lula was beginning to believe it down to her very soul.

"If you don't want to see what I'm doing, if you don't approve, then don't watch me. I won't give you advice about Harland, if you don't give me any about Barton." Lula raised her chin in defiance like she'd seen her sister Hattie do when she was younger. Hattie had been a terribly defiant child.

"I won't give you any such bargain. I will not watch you throw your life away. You mean too much to me, Lula."

Chapter Fifteen

The huge bush didn't provide quite enough cover for Barton to pace as he wanted to. It was too dark to see his watch but it felt as if he'd waited there for hours. Would she ever get there?

At supper, he couldn't keep his eyes off Lula. She'd sat with Izzy and one other woman, and though she'd done her best to avoid looking at him, their gazes had caught often. Then Izzy had frowned at him and forced Lula to switch seats so that her back was facing him. If only they didn't have to be so secretive.

Sparks in Spearfish

What he felt for Lula wasn't dirty or wrong, hiding it made it that way. It was as if by holding back, when he *did* see her, he had to release all that he felt and it overwhelmed them both.

The soft rustle of skirts and the click of heeled boots drew him out from his spot. There she was, under the lamplight just yards away. His Lula. He could think of her no other way. She glanced this way, then that, finally rushing over to the bush as he pulled her into the small secluded corner of the building and right into his arms.

She fit perfectly to his chest and clung to him as he'd been praying she would for years. This woman, this moment, was an answer to all those mumbled supplications of a boy lost in his affection for a girl who he thought would never see him as more than a nuisance.

He stood, waiting for her to break the hold, because he didn't want to. He'd hold her until eternity came, if she'd let him. When she did pull away, he cupped her face in his hands, the softness of her cheeks warmed every part of him, and he took in every inch of her in the dark. Her golden hair caught bits of moonlight, and her pearly white skin glowed.

The temptation was too much, he bent, pressing his lips to hers, and she responded in kind. He had to be closer to her, to feel her. His hand delved into her soft hair and he couldn't stop a moan from escaping. How he loved her hair. The curling softness beneath his work-roughed hands excited every part of him.

Lula clutched at the back of his vest and arched her back. He let his lips roam down to her neck where the fashionable high collared shirt she wore was in his way. He tugged against it, to get at the tender sweetness of her neck as Lula trailed kisses down his own jaw. What was he doing? They were in the middle of the school and could both be seen any moment, not to mention where his thoughts were headed. Sweet mercy!

"Lula," he drew away from her and held her shoulders to steady himself and his resolve to stop before they went too far. "We can't do this. It isn't wrong, please don't think it is, but only after we are secured to one another. And I want that, more than you know, but I can't ruin you."

She reached for him and held tight, her hands bunched his shirt and her chest still heaved, breathless from his kiss. Even in the night, her lips were dark with his ministrations, and he wanted to taste them again.

Her voice quavered. "I don't know what to do. I can't stand to be away from you, but when I'm near you, it's as if I can't even control who I am. All my thoughts rush to you and I can't do simple things. Izzy is suspicious and will be watching our every move. Harland, too, has already told her he would be watching us closely. I don't want to lose who I am, but I fear I'm already lost."

Her words split his heart in two, and he drew her into his chest, cradling her gently. Her body quaked and a sob tore from her throat.

"I'm so sorry, Lula. I never meant to do this to you. Why is it that I'm always hurting you? No matter if I try to get your attention by tugging on your hair or pulling you close, it still hurts you. I can't do this. I can't hurt you anymore."

She clung to him. "Don't you dare. You can't leave me. I can't do this without you. I thought I could, but I can't."

"You always have, Lula. You are so strong, so beautiful, and intelligent, you can do this. I can't leave this position. I've promised them the remainder of this year. For the remainder of this year, we can't meet. No matter how much I want to. And I *do* want to."

Lula shuddered against him and tipped her head. "I can't, Barton." She brushed her lips on his and the fire he'd doused flamed back at him. "You must." He backed himself against the wall, away from her. Putting distance between them. "I didn't ask you out here to woo you away from your purity. On the contrary, I want you to be a pure bride for me. I asked you out here to ask you if you would join me in Spearfish. But I know now what a mistake that would be. I can't be alone with you."

She took a step toward him, closing the gap, and he held his breath. If he could keep from kissing her again, he'd not go further. Heaven help him. She stopped and bowed her head slightly. "I'll do my best, Barton. But I fear I will fail. You've started something in me I don't know how to control or contain. How will I ever teach now? This temptation is a fire and it's just as consuming as if we'd actually coupled. I can't look at you without thinking of your lips on mine. I can't be near you without wanting your hands on me. I am jealous of your every glance. How? How can I move on and be a teacher when my heart knows this is what I will give up?"

There was no good answer for her. He wanted her there just so he could see her, but at the same time, she was far too much of a temptation. Her brother-in-law was an honorable man and if he'd gone the way his own thoughts and body had wanted to go, he would've been forced to admit to everyone that he was no leader. He'd led a student astray.

Lula rushed out from behind the bush. Her finger's still felt the crispness of his shirt and her lips still burned with the stubble of his jaw. She'd turned wanton. He'd met her with a kiss and she'd practically dragged him to the ground. What must he think of her? She'd tried to confess her growing love for him, but it had come across just as she'd been, needy. Desirous of only the feelings and nothing deeper, but deeper was what she desired most of all. Though Barton had been a classmate for two years, because of what he'd done, she didn't know him well. And now, she couldn't. He was forbidden. He'd as much as told her he couldn't go near her outside of class. Within class, she had to act accordingly.

Izzy would be happy, she'd get to keep Lula nearby and get her wish to see Lula stay away from Barton, but those things she'd said, couldn't be true. Barton had shown his heart tonight. He wasn't that boy who'd coated her pencil with tobacco juice so it was sticky, leaving her hands a dark gold. He wasn't the boy who'd tugged on the tie of her petticoat when it stuck above the waistline of her skirt to laugh when it fell off and tripped her. And she was beginning to see just who that boy was, because he hadn't changed as Izzy said. He'd just taken aim differently. Barton had wanted her attention from that very first day, and she'd given it to him in spades. Where he was concerned, she'd always given him just what he'd asked of her. If only he'd simply *asked* her back then.

If he had, where would she be now? Certainly not at a school for teaching. If she and Barton were together, he'd be away at school while she was at home, alone. His antics didn't seem quite so terrible in that light.

As she pushed open the door to her room, Izzy bolted out of her chair with a gasp. "Lula! My word. What have you done?"

What could possibly show on her face? Lula looked down at herself and, though she was a little rumpled, nothing looked particularly out of place. Izzy stomped up to her and tugged on her neckline, now hanging loose near her collar. When had that happened?

Lula stepped back and closed the door then leaned against it. "Izzy, the rest of the year is going to be the hardest thing I've ever done and I need your help to get through it. Please don't hold what I've done against me. My old dreams are dying as new ones form, but I can't act on them."

"New dreams? What if he leaves you? What if you give up your dream, and lose him? Then you have nothing left. He's given you no guarantees. He's given you nothing..." She tugged on Lula's neckline again, "except for things that could get you in trouble. This isn't good or right, Lula. Please, don't do this. I don't want to see him hurt you yet again."

"I'm trying to keep everything under control. Don't be angry with me. This isn't what it seems. I've gained him and lost him all in a few minutes, just be understanding." Lula drew the neck of her shirt closed and buttoned it back up.

"It's exactly what it seems. You will turn into your sister Hattie if you keep on this path. You were headed toward a quiet, sweet life as a teacher, but if you keep dallying with that...charlatan, you will end up a harlot."

The words pierced her. "What a vile thing to say. You know nothing about what happened and only a little of my sister. I'm not Hattie." While she loved Hattie, and her sister had worked so hard to be redeemed, Lula still didn't want to end up like her. Even now, Hattie was just a wife. A woman who had nothing left of herself beyond Hugh. When her husband entered a room, Hattie had no attention left for anyone else. How could she allow that to be her destiny? Did her blood really determine just who she was, did it matter what she did to try to change her own life? She'd thrown herself in Barton's arms, and hadn't wanted to let go, even when he'd pulled away. He was stronger than her.

"Vile or not, it needed to be said to put your head in order. Are you going to leave? I think it would be the safest. One slip and you could destroy both of you. Are you willing to do that?"

The tears that had welled behind her eyes since she'd left Barton spilled over. Izzy had always been so understanding. She needed a friend, not a mother. "I can't do anything else besides teach, and I can't leave him."

Izzy backed away and crossed her arms. "Then you must do what I'm doing and continue working. Stay away from him if this is what happens when you're together. I told you at the beginning of the year he had plans for you. You have to decide if he's worth giving up everything for...or if your goal, the one you made so you could be independent, is what matters most. You can't have both."

Chapter Sixteen

As Lula stepped into the classroom, Izzy yanked her into the seat in front of her at the back of the room, toppling her into the hard chair.

"Don't you dare put yourself up there," she hissed through clenched teeth.

Was that how it would be, Izzy constantly controlling her every move? Lula sat at her desk and arranged her books and papers. Barton sat in his desk at the front, head down. The set of his shoulders, tense and strong, told her he knew she was in the room, was noting her without looking up.

Sparks in Spearfish

The class began and his glance swept the room and skipped over her. It hit her like a slap. He couldn't even look at her. Had her behavior the night before behind the bush tarnished his thoughts of her forever?

He stood and leaned over his desk, his strong jaw steady as he began the lecture. The same jaw she'd kissed. At the memory of his hands roaming to her neck and pulling down her collar to nuzzle her in ways she'd never dreamed about, heat seeped up her high neckline. She had to stop, wanting him before they were wed was wrong. What if they never were? That was why purity was expected. Until two people committed and said their oath before God, anything could happen. His thoughts of her could cool and she would be alone, in fact, if all they felt went no deeper than the attraction between them, it would be better if they did separate.

The black board filled as the day wore on and Lula tried to focus. He would quiz everyone before the end of class and she would most certainly fail. Nothing would get past her own thoughts. Being with him was too fresh, new, exciting. And now she couldn't spend even a moment with him, sharpening the ache in her belly the more he entered her thoughts.

Barton called on Izzy to come to the front to write on the board. He'd never call on *her* again because it would draw attention to her. A strange tension hung over the classroom as if everyone knew something was wrong, but couldn't place. Every student searched each face for the source and Lula prayed they skimmed by her just as Barton had.

The clock struck the hour and Barton dismissed everyone. Izzy grappled Lula's arm and lifted her from the chair. "Don't you dare give him the chance to talk to you. You've done well so far, just keep going." Izzy tossed a glare at him over her shoulder. Lula turned, hoping he would look up from his desk, that he would at least acknowledge her in an otherwise empty room, but his focus stayed on his notes. His head slightly bent and lips flat.

Izzy's footfalls echoed down the hall as she stomped her way to the exit. "There. You made it through the hardest day. It wasn't so difficult, was it? You can do this, and before you know it, you will wonder why you were ever drawn to..." She lowered her voice to a conspiratorial whisper,

"Barton Oleson." At least she wasn't living by two separate rules. Izzy didn't want her to get caught but wasn't making a silly mistake like announcing her folly in front of everyone.

"I don't think you understand. That was one of the most difficult days I've ever gone through. In the past, I could go to him if he acted like he did today and ask him what was wrong. Not now, I *know* what's wrong. Me. He's disgusted with me, but still has to have me sitting there."

"He has no reason to be. You're the one who should be disgusted. What he did to you! No gentleman does that. Harland would *never* do that."

It was easy to recall exactly what she'd done and felt, but she wouldn't confess it to Izzy. If she did, she'd be on the first train back home. Izzy would consider her a hussy, report her to the dean, and Lula would go home. Her brother-in-law, Beau, and her sister, Ruby, would be so disappointed in her. She couldn't let them down, even if she'd let herself down. She'd let herself become Hattie in thought, if not in deed, but she could still be redeemed. If Hattie could find peace and healing, so could Lula. Except that she didn't want to give up her dream. She didn't want to live for someone else's pleasure. There was more to life than doting.

Every single one of her older sisters had found happiness and love with unexpected men. And every last one of them adored their husbands, but not like Hattie and Hugh. Though, he also was rather oblivious to the world when Hattie was around. Perhaps that was just the way they were? She'd have to find out over Christmas break. She'd be going home and could closely watch her three oldest sisters, Ruby, Jennie, and Hattie, with their husbands. Her other two sisters now lived elsewhere. Eva, Hattie's twin, lived in Lead with her husband, and Frances lived in Deadwood with her husband, Clive. They wrote dime romance novels together, though no one knew that but family.

Lula's steps slowed, making Izzy stumble. "I want to go back. I want to talk to him."

Izzy pulled harder. "No. I won't let you do that. He did well. He ignored you. Take a cue from him and be good."

That was the hardest thing in the

world to be.

The last two weeks had been torturous. His lovely Lula had to sit by as he called on everyone else, as he talked with everyone else. She'd steadily folded under his lack of attention, like a dying flower, and it was killing him. At the end of the first week, he'd been helping the other students write an essay about the Civil War. He'd stopped at every desk and made comments or helped them in some way. But when he'd gotten to hers, he couldn't do it. Couldn't make himself look into those beautiful blue eyes and just talk. Not after a week of separation.

Those blue eyes had been hopeful, she'd had her paper at the ready. Then he'd walked right by, and he'd crushed her. Her eyes had turned glassy, reflecting the bright light pouring in the windows, and he'd prayed she wouldn't cry. He couldn't stand to see her cry, never could. Not even when he'd tormented her. Her tears were precious and no one better make her shed one, not even him.

Though the class had fallen back into its normal routine and feel, he couldn't quite force himself back to normal. Lula belonged at the front with him. He needed her smile of encouragement. He needed to lose his place in his notes because he thought he'd heard a noise she'd made. While the utter distraction of Lula was gone with her in the back of the room, his teaching was more rote, less inviting. Even he could sense it.

His male students had wondered about Lula without asking, but now, after two weeks without incident, they had forgotten about her strange behavior, and his. Though, he couldn't put it all on Lula. He'd had very little discretion when the term had started. His roommate's warning of the danger of being dismissed had done the trick and, obviously, his warning to Lula had done the same. It had worked too well. He truly never saw her. Not even in the cafeteria. Where she ate, he had no idea, but it wasn't where he could catch a glimpse of her.

Every day that passed was one day closer to Christmas break. Lula had never gone home in past years, so she might stay this time and now, he could stay as well. He could get caught up with learning lessons from professor Cook and still have time to spend some evenings with Lula. He needed to hold her, to wipe the tears he'd caused from her eyes, to tell her he missed her.

He couldn't do that just yet. The scene behind the bush was still too fresh. He'd gone too far and he'd never put her, put *them*, in that position again. His pa had warned him that the right woman would not only put a fire in his blood, but a fire in his soul. His pa was right. Lula was as hot as the sun and she would burn for no one but him. But he had to do things in the right order. He had to get finished with this year, speak with her brother-in-law, and then ask for her hand.

First, he had to get through the next few months. Just until the holidays. There had to be something he could do for her, some way to let her know how he felt and that he was counting down the days until they could be together. Christmas marked the halfway point in the year. Once through that, he could get through the last bit. He just needed the respite of spending time with her when no one from the school would be around to witness them.

The papers from that day's work lay across his desk and he gathered them all up. Lula had steadily been getting worse and worse. Her focus was off, she wasn't giving him her best work and, as he'd feared, it was getting difficult to be fair in grading her papers. He couldn't keep up the act much longer or it would affect her ability once she was out teaching students. If she ever had to.

How could he call himself a teacher and not be fair with each student? But this troubled soul was his Lula and her trouble was all his fault. What could he do? The red pencil used for correcting sat at the top of his desk in a cutout groove. The first paper he glanced at was fine and he marked it. It was boring, but completely expected. Each paper was much of the same, and he worked his way down the short stack quickly, finally getting to Lula's. He'd grown accustomed to doing hers last.

The words across the top broke his heart. *Just fail me. I'm ready to go home, but I can't leave without an excuse. I can't stand that you hate me so much that you can't even look at me. Please. Just send me home. Lula Arnsby*

No. He wouldn't send her home and he couldn't. How could she think, for a moment, that he hated her? Far from it, he was fairly drunk with her. She had to stay and be a teacher for his plans to succeed. If she went home, he'd never see her again. There wasn't another teacher school nearby and he had no reason to ever go to Deadwood.

He couldn't fail her. How could she have handed that in to him to force his hand? There was literally nothing else on the page besides her note. He picked up the pencil and jotted his own response. *Miss Arnsby, You're better than this. Please complete the sheet and return to my office for a grade. Mr. Oleson.*

How he hated being so impersonal when it was so obvious she needed him. He said a prayer that he could handle himself and stay behind his desk. Unless she wouldn't come to see him... Would she continue to force him into failing her by not doing as he asked? He clenched his jaw as he considered telling her that he didn't hate her. Quite the opposite, his heart ached for her. It was something he needed to tell her in person, not in a note that could be seen by others. He tossed it on his stack.

Teaching was never what he'd wanted to do, but even this, that he'd done for Lula, had turned into something that hurt her. Would he ever make things right between them and have her love him?

Chapter Seventeen

Barton wouldn't fail her. After two weeks of sitting in his class and watching him from the back of the room. Seeing his eyes glance to each student and waiting for her turn so she could at least share that moment with him, and having him skip over her. Trying not to cry when he walked past her desk after visiting with every other student. Surely that was even more noticeable than a quick chat about her paper would be?

That's when she'd given up. Barton hated her. He couldn't even stand to look at her. His lack of attention had made her feel dirty for their time behind the bush. It wasn't his load to carry, he'd given her a kiss, she'd tempted him further. It had shown him just the kind of woman she was inside, and it must have disgusted him. How else could he so blithely ignore her?

Then his note on the sheet she'd gotten that morning, the one where she'd been sure he'd fail her so she could go home, had come back to her, admonishing her. Why couldn't he just fail her? Didn't he realize the torture this was, every single day? Watching him, knowing she couldn't trust herself to say a word, wanting to crumple to her desk in a pile of tears at the end of every day. And he wanted her to stay.

She'd stared at his words, not sharing them with anyone. It had been strange to have him hand back the papers and not one of the students, but now she knew why. He wouldn't want anyone else to see that note and know that what should've gotten a failing grade, he'd given her another chance. A chance she didn't deserve, or at this point, particularly want.

Lula scribbled a few lines on the sheet and left Izzy in the room. After a week of quiet, Izzy had given up on mothering her. It hadn't worked anyway. Her constant attention had only made Lula feel worse about what she'd done. Ruby, her sister that had acted as her mother for eight years, would frown at her and be just as motherly. Izzy reminded Lula of what she would return home to. Izzy treated her as if she wore scarlet and painted her lips. She could've just as well given herself to Barton; the guilt wouldn't be any less.

Campus was dark as she made her way to the administration building. Barton didn't have an office to himself, but he did have a desk with other teachers and there was a room there where people could talk in private to avoid disturbing others. It was late enough in the evening that he wouldn't be there, and if he was, he'd be alone. Heat built at her center and tingled outward as she approached.

She climbed the stairs to the teacher offices and pushed open the door, letting it close silently behind her. As she'd thought, the room was fairly dark, except for one lamp on a desk in the middle of the room, where Barton sat hunched over his desk. His head was in his hands. He looked so very tired. Her fingers ached to rub his shoulders and soothe away the pain of his day as she'd seen Ruby do for Beau. If only he would let her. But she couldn't touch him, couldn't speak to him, couldn't look at him. Not if she was to act as he'd treated her.

The paper crumpled in her hands and he started, looking up at her. "Lula...you're here..."

Hadn't he asked her to come? Should she hand him her paper and leave. Now that he saw her and had spoken her name, her heart tore, once again, and she wanted to cry. Her jaw trembled under the weight of the emotion. What had she given up, destroyed? She blinked away the tears gathering in her lashes as she strode forward and thrust the sheet at him. His hand reached for hers but she backed away. If he touched her, she would melt again. She would become the wanton woman within herself she'd grown to hate. The one Izzy had shown her as bad, filthy, evil.

He glanced down at the paper as she steadily backed away. He wouldn't like that she'd ignored his request, had still turned in the page undone. But only as her teacher, not as someone who cared about her. She'd laid her heart bare for him in her note and he hadn't bothered to respond. A scholastic response from a teacher was all she should ever expect, but she'd desired so much more.

She'd made it to the door when he glanced back up at her, his eyes full of pain. "Why do you want to leave, Lula? I don't understand. I can't do this, why are you asking me to?"

Did he expect her to bare her soul once again? Hadn't she done that enough? Hadn't she told him just how she felt?

"I can't stay here another minute." She spun to open the door and strong hands wrapped around her and stayed her hands.

"You shouldn't be here." His warm breath on her ear and neck ignited the flame she'd tried so hard to prove didn't exist in her. Because if it did, it made her a harlot. She'd desired that feeling again and it was wrong.

"I'm trying to go, but you won't let me." She couldn't move; cocooned in his arms with his hands over hers on the door.

"Every day I watch you and see you hurting, and I want to hold you and wipe away every tear, and I can't. But I can't send you home. What if you cry there and I never know about it, what if I never see you again?

What if you leave and never come back? I can't live without you, Lula." Every breath fanned the flame, every word a bit of kindling until the inferno inside would consume her.

"You've already said you can't have me. You're torturing me, Barton. You're forcing me to stay here to sit and watch you every day when I can never talk to you, never look at you, never touch you, or kiss you, or hold you. Never. I don't have the strength to keep going. Send me home. Set me free." Though leaving and never seeing him again would hurt even more, at least she didn't have to have the fresh tearing of her heart when he passed her by another day.

"I won't." He mumbled into her neck. Even against her shirtwaist, his mouth was hot on her shoulder, and she hated herself for not only enjoying it, but wanting more. She could go nowhere, he'd trapped her there.

"You've either got to let me go or let me turn, but you can't do this to me. You can't push me away, then kiss me…"

He gently spun her around to face him, his blue eyes soft and warm on her face. How she wanted to kiss the frown lines near his eyes, the lines that, before, crinkled in his smile. He'd asked her to give up her dream to be with him, had hinted that was what he wanted, so what was keeping him from sending her home? If he would just fail her, they could be together.

Still inflamed by his kisses on her shoulder, she knew. Izzy had been right. He would push her as far as he could, then he would turn back into the boy she'd known and laugh at her.

Barton opened his mouth to speak, then leaned into her just a fraction of an inch from her lips. She wanted his kiss, but wouldn't that lead her down the same path they'd walked just two weeks ago? The one that had led to so much hurt. He wouldn't push her farther, she wouldn't let him, and it was his kiss that started it all. She forced her hands to his chest and held firm, stopping him.

"You wouldn't want to kiss me if you knew my heart." The leather scent that always surrounded him filled her. His breathing ragged as he closed his eyes.

"I do know your heart. I've gotten to know all about you over the last two years. Did you think I would do all of this for some brief lust? I'm not a boy anymore. You're in my blood, Lula, and I don't expect I'll ever be able to separate you from me, and I don't want to."

"How can you know anything about me? You spent two whole years tormenting me." She'd never said a word to him before this year that hadn't been forced from her lips. He couldn't know anything about her.

He took a step closer, his mouth so near. "I know that you can't stand to be the center of attention. You don't like people watching you, so I always thought you were brave to want to become a teacher. I know that you have a tender heart, easily crushed, and that your tears used to come very easy. You got stronger by your second year. I was so proud of you for fighting back against me, but that wasn't what I wanted. I never wanted to be the one you hated, but if I could make you think about me, that was all that mattered. I came back this year just for you, Lula. This, teaching, was never my purpose. But I couldn't let you go. I know that I broke you and keep breaking you, and I'm so sorry that I have to ask you to stay, to keep this up. But,

I can't let you go. Maybe I'm not as strong as you, but I've done all this, come all this way. I won't do it."

She couldn't listen to another word. Now that he'd opened up and told her how he felt, she wanted to turn it off. He knew her better, knew about her, and she knew very little about him.

"I spent so much time trying to hate you, I never learned who you were, as a man."

He closed his eyes as a soft groan escaped his lips. Though she couldn't leave, he was not pressed against her and she wanted the weight of him; solid, strong, reassuring. But if she did, it would be the invitation he was looking for, the invitation that would lead to... Her naive mind couldn't fill in what would happen.

"I want you too much, Lula. I can't do this. I can't meet with you here. You are too beautiful and I don't want to hurt you. Not anymore than I already have." He bent and kissed her cheek, so softly, then his lips brushed hers like the whisper of silk, and she held her breath to keep from bursting. He reached behind her, holding her to him for just a moment, then pulled the door behind her as he stepped back, taking her with him in his dance. Once the door was open, he spun her away from him. "Go. And don't ask me to fail you again. I'll quit this job before I do that."

Chapter Eighteen

Izzy's parents bustled about the small room, collecting her bags and blankets. They'd traveled to come get her along with a few of her brothers, though they waited outside, to take her home for the holiday. Lula sat to the side, out of the way. The room was far too small for her to be of much help, and the friendship she'd so cherished had been fractured.

She'd steadily gotten her assignments done as Barton had asked, but her heart was long gone from the work. She'd never teach and she knew it. Her family's expectation, along with Barton's request, kept her there. Her work was poor, but she didn't care. Though he occasionally wrote a personal note to her on the top of her papers, he rarely even looked at her.

Harland's friend, Amos, had told Izzy that he'd like to take Lula for ice cream or to walk about town, but she didn't want to. It would mean leaving town, walking, talking with others, and being with a man who wasn't Barton. There was nothing that would make her want to go with others. Even Barton. She wanted him all to herself, not in a class, not in town, but to talk and be with him. It was as if her very soul was thirsty for his company.

He'd stood in front of the classroom week after week, doing his job and doing it well. How could he continue on, do what he needed to do, and not feel the empty hole she couldn't avoid? He'd thought her stronger than him, but it was a lie. She was weak.

Since he hadn't want to talk with her or see her, she didn't need to tell him, she wasn't coming back. Her brother-in-law, Beau, was coming the next day to get her. She'd already packed her whole trunk, when Izzy had been at dinner the day before, and she wasn't going to return to the Normal School. If he couldn't send her away, she'd make the decision for him.

The letter she'd written to Barton had been the hardest thing she'd ever done, and even now, she didn't want to post it. If anyone saw it but him, she'd be ruined. But he had to know. He had to know that she loved him. There were no other words for it. It wasn't just lust, she wanted more than the warmth of his touch, she wanted the comfort of his strength, the sweetness of his smile, his leadership. What he'd done to her in the past was gone, redeemed for good, forgotten. In its place now sat an empty hole, that Barton couldn't fill, because he wasn't willing.

She'd told him where to find her in case he ever changed his mind, but she didn't expect him to. How could he look at her as a wife, a good and faithful companion, when they'd shared nothing but heat and passion? It wasn't possible. He'd spoke of wanting, of needing, but not of a future. Not really. They had none. If she left, he'd never follow, if she stayed, it would break her.

Izzy rushed back into the room and pulled Lula to her feet, crushing her in a quick faltering embrace. "I'll see you in a few weeks. Rest. You need it. The end of the year is even harder than the first and I'll need you!"

Her response choked in her throat. She couldn't tell Izzy, not now when she was about to leave. Izzy would go on just fine and be a wonderful teacher, or wife, dependent on Harland. "I'll see you." It was the most she could say and not lie. She hoped she would see Izzy again, someday.

Beau arrived the next morning with the buckboard and lifted her trunk down the stairs. He hadn't said a word about it. Since she'd never gone home for the Christmas break, she'd hoped he would think it was normal.

Barton rushed out of the administration building and her heart stopped, then skipped into a run. No one else would be taking their whole trunk home, would he notice? Would he say anything to Beau? She shrank back, hoping Barton wouldn't see her behind her brother-in-law's thick shoulders.

No such luck. Barton smiled as he approached Beau and held out his hand for a quick shake.

"Mr. Rockford, good to finally meet you."

Beau nodded. "The same."

Lula almost laughed. So many people were put off by Beau and his tendency to speak little, listen more.

"Sir. I'm currently Lula's teacher, though that wasn't intentional, her professor had a terrible accident a few months back and he's only just now getting back on his feet. He's hoping to take over teaching again after the holiday."

Lula gasped. If she were coming back, it would've only taken one paper to accomplish her goal with the professor. He would've given her a failing grade where Barton had refused.

Beau stopped and leaned against the wagon. "That so?"

Barton looked the part of her teacher with his lean-fitting black trousers, crisp white shirt and black tie. She wanted to be on his arm, to have him claim her. Who wouldn't want to have a man like that?

"Lula and I have gotten to know each other a bit better over the first half of the year and, if you've got the spare space, even in the barn, I'd like to visit over the holiday. I'll sure miss her while she's gone."

No, he couldn't be doing this. If he was visiting, she'd have to admit to him face to face that she wasn't returning. What would he say? Would he convince her family to insist she return? He couldn't do this to her. She found herself shaking her head as Beau looked to her.

"Lula? There's always the Bradley place he can stay in if you'd like him to visit. You know what we expect of you."

The look on Barton's face, so expectant. How could she deny him? But she had to. As she continued to slowly shake her head, his face fell. Her words trapped somewhere in her throat and she blinked to keep away the tears. Why would he want to come see her? He hadn't allowed them to be together for months and she'd ached for him. What good would it do at her home? Heat crawled up her neck as she realized they were both waiting for her reply.

"Wouldn't you want to visit your own family, Barton?" She gasped as Beau's eyebrows rose at her use of Mr. Oleson's first name. She should've used his proper name, since he was her teacher.

"No. My family isn't expecting me, so if I don't visit you, I'm afraid I'll be all alone."

He couldn't be left alone with only the younger students. As much as she didn't want him with her, it wouldn't be fair. He was pulling on her heartstrings once again.

"Then you are welcome."

He smiled and shook hands with Beau once again. "I'll just grab my pack and my horse. It'll only take a few minutes."

Beau nodded. "Take your time. I'd like to talk to Lula and it might take a bit."

She'd known that was coming. Of course, he'd want to talk to her. She'd acted like a love-sick fool, and maybe she was.

As Barton strode back toward the administration building, Beau turned to face her. "Lula? I wasn't born yesterday. Teachers aren't allowed to step out with students, and no woman teacher is allowed to be married. We talked about this before you even applied to Spearfish. Now, I know you were young when you made that choice. Sixteen is young to decide you don't want to wed, but it makes no sense to me why we'd pay for schooling that you're never going to use if you're interested in this man enough to say he can visit."

It was more words than she'd heard him string together for her in longer than she could remember. And she owed him the truth. He *was* paying for her classes and they needed her at home. "Truth be told, I don't know. I *feel* all sorts of things, but I'm so confused... I wanted to go home to talk to Ruby and Hattie. I need to know..." Why couldn't she form the words? Beau had always acted as a good father, but he was just that, a father, a protector. She didn't need that now, she needed someone to talk with about matters of the heart. Barton was who she wanted to protect her now. Beau had lost his place.

"If you change your mind, it wouldn't be good to send him out on his own with just a horse, so you tell him now if you don't want him there. I don't want to have to worry about him."

Did she want to tell him no, or pray that they finally got the chance to talk when he was with her for the few weeks of the Christmas holiday. What would come of it? There was no chance of them being alone at home, so she could talk with him without the pressure of wanting his touch. It wouldn't be possible.

"I don't want him to be alone. I want to see him, I just also want to talk about how I feel with Hattie and Ruby."

Beau raised that horrible eyebrow one last time. "And that trunk? What's that for? I may be a man, but I know you don't need all that for two weeks."

Her sisters had warned her about trying to pull one over on Beau. It never worked. He was too smart, too observant, and he loved each of them so much.

"That's what I wanted to talk to my sisters about." It wasn't completely a lie, though just an hour ago, there would've been no way her sisters could've talked her out of staying home. Now, the one she'd have to worry about, was Barton.

He'd almost missed Lula. If he hadn't been watching some of his other students leaving out his window, he'd have missed Beau driving up, and worse, he'd have missed seeing him lug that huge trunk down to the buckboard. Why hadn't he seen that move coming? Lula had been begging him to fail her, to let her go home. The Christmas holiday was the perfect chance for her to leave and never return. Fortunately, it was also the perfect chance for him to visit her in a place where talking to her was perfectly acceptable and where they'd be surrounded at all times by her family. Somewhere he'd have to behave himself. There was more at risk at her home because if he turned Beau against him, he'd never marry Lula. But if everything went well, he could ask for her hand sooner than he'd planned.

He threw a couple clean shirts and trousers into a saddle bag along with anything else he could think to grab. Professor Cook would be surprised when he didn't show up later that day, but it couldn't be helped. He'd been there for months, without fail. His time as teacher was coming to an end and he'd be ready for an actual teaching position of his own if he didn't choose to remain as the assistant. That would depend on Lula. If she would marry him, he wouldn't look back. If she wanted to go back to the school or if her family insisted that she return, he would go back to being just the assistant for the remainder of the year.

The saddle bag sat heavy over his shoulder as he rushed to the stable for Star. He saddled her quickly and led her out to where Beau and Lula waited by their rig.

Beau nodded to him. "It's not a hard ride, just long. We'll stop at least once along the way."

He patted Star's neck and mounted, ready to find out even more about Lula and her life outside of Spearfish, meet her sisters who meant so much to her, and see the ranch that she loved. But most of all, just to spend time with her. How he'd missed her.

Two hours later, after suppressing the urge to talk to Lula the whole way, he followed Beau and his wagon up a hill to the Ferguson Ranch. It sat perched at the top with a wide flat area for one large ranch house, two smaller homes, a huge barn, and a fence that led down the hill. It was beautiful, so much like his home in Belle Fourche. As much as he missed his own ma and pa, they would always be there, he could visit them anytime. He had to do this, the whole rest of his life depended on it.

He dismounted and was right there to help Lula down from her seat on the wagon bench. Beau eyed him for a moment, but he caught the look of appreciation. There wasn't a father he'd ever met that wasn't big on respect.

Lula's arm quivered under his hand and he squeezed it. Beau climbed down from his seat and came around to them.

"Lula, why don't you show Barton where he can store his horse and tack? I'll get your trunk moved into the house."

He'd meant to ask Lula about that very thing, but would she clamp her mouth shut as soon as he asked? Would it be better to let her tell him about why she'd tried to run from him? Every word had become complicated and weighted; he'd hurt her so badly.

Lula said not a word and took Star's reins toward the barn. He followed close behind. The creak of the trunk being lifted from the back of the wagon was soon drowned out by the various sounds of the stable.

Star bobbed her head high and Lula reached around, grabbing her halter and speaking softly. Star calmed and followed her to a stall near the back.

"If you tell me where everything

is, I can take care of her. You probably want to go on in and see your family. You probably miss them."

She looped the reins around the front of the stall for him then rested her hand on Star's flank as she made her way back out of the stall. "I do want to see them, but I can't just leave you out here. I should show you were you can take your things, where you'll be staying." Her voice quivered. It was chilly, but he was sure that wasn't it.

"I'll be here for a bit. Go on. They'll want to see you." But he didn't want her to leave. He'd been far too long without her. Just being near her set every muscle in his body ablaze.

"You just got here and you're trying to get rid of me already?"

That hadn't been his intention at all. "No, I just..." What? Wanted to hold her, talk to her, keep her. But if he did that, was selfish with her, she'd never have a chance to see her family.

Lula stepped toward him, then another tentative step. When had she become so unsure of herself? Had he expected too much of her and given not enough?

He spread his arms and prayed she wouldn't shun him, wouldn't run anywhere but to him. She sobbed and rushed to his arms, clinging to him. "I've missed you."

They'd been in each other's presence every single day but he could honestly say he'd missed her, too. He pressed a kiss to the top of her head. "Why, Lula? Why would you leave me?"

She moved to pull away but he couldn't let her go, not yet. He held her tightly to him and brushed her hair from her face. "I told you. I couldn't stand it anymore. What I'd done. It was horrible. Unforgivable. You couldn't even look at me." She tried again to dodge from him, her shame heating the cheek under the tips of his fingers.

"No, dear Lula. No. You couldn't shame me. I couldn't look on you because I wanted to spend every moment with you that I could and I wasn't allowed. If you left, I'd never see you again. I couldn't let you leave and yet, seeing you every day was such a torture."

She rested her head to his chest, her soft curls catching in the stubble he'd meant to shave that morning, but had ended up leaving instead.

"What do you hope to happen here?" Her words were muffled into the fabric of his coat.

"I hope to spend as much time with you as you as your family will allow. I hope to convince you to give me one more chance, and I hope to talk with you about what our future might look like."

She gasped and, again, he had to hold her from pulling away from him. He could hold her to him forever, but at least until her quaking stopped. "I didn't think we had a future. I was so afraid."

"I can't think of a future with anyone but you, Buttercup."

Chapter Nineteen

They had spent six glorious days together, talking, walking, holding hands. All the things that couples do when they are courting and not having to hide it from the world. Barton didn't ever want to go back. How could he? He was growing to like the easy way Lula's hand fit in his as they walked the trails around the ranch. How her eyes lingered on his face even after they'd finished a sentence and neither of them had words left. He adored every part of her.

Barton led her to the sofa and waited for her to sit and arrange her skirts so he wouldn't sit on them.

Christmas was tomorrow and he was still unsure how he should handle it. He sat next to her and she reached for his hand, blushing sweetly, as if just holding his hand were precious to her—and he hoped it was. As he took her hand, she tucked it under the folds of her skirt, bringing a quick laugh to his lips.

"We don't have to hide here." Once the next few months was finished, he'd never hide his love for her again.

A soft smile warmed her beautiful lips, lips he hadn't allowed himself to taste in far too long. "I know, but it seems we've spent so much of our time together hiding..."

"I don't want to hide anymore, Lula. It's killing us both. The hiding left you thinking I was ashamed of you and I never was." If he hadn't been holding her hand, he'd have allowed himself to trail his fingers down her soft cheek, but he wouldn't let go of her until she willed it. This whole visit was about her, and convincing her with his actions that he could be the man she needed him to be.

"But, if I go back as a student, we'll be right back where we were. Even if the professor returns, we can't talk. Even sitting near you would lead to speculation. We can't even do anything now, because if you marry before your term is up, to one of your students, they could take away your student teacher certificate. Then, what would we do? We'd be two teachers...who couldn't teach anywhere."

As much as he hated to admit she was right, everything she said was true. He opened his mouth to ask her what she thought when Ruby entered the room. "Good. I'm glad you're both here. Nora has Joseph out playing in the snow and the others are all out working"

Lula loosened her grip on his hand, but didn't let go. She was giving him the chance to release her if he wanted to. Instead he held tighter and gave her a quick smile. He wouldn't leave her.

Ruby glanced at him for a moment, then fixed her gaze on Lula. "We've had a chance to talk about school, but I think now is a good time to include Barton in the conversation. I think he needs to know your worries, fears, and feelings."

Lula stood quickly, dropping his hand, and paced the room. He'd never seen her do that. "It isn't that I don't want to tell him, Ruby. It's just that, all of those things don't matter. They just complicate everything further."

"No." Barton stood and stopped her movement. Her worry poured off of her, right to his heart. "I need to know. Your decisions matter to my life. From now on, everything matters, and I want to know."

How could he make any decision without knowing what it would do to her? Hadn't he tried that up until now with disastrous results?

She tucked her head and searched the space between them for the words, finally looking up into his eyes. "Barton...I love you. I don't want to go back to school at all, but if you or my sisters require it, I will."

Could he ask her to go through another four months of sitting in that desk for no reason? If she was never going to teach, why should she? Because he couldn't bear four months without seeing her.

"I don't want to make you, and I won't. But I love you, Lula, and I don't think I can go without you that long."

Ruby separated the two of them and held each by the arm. "If you both love each other, then you can wait. But you must understand the temptations that will be there."

It wasn't his place to tell Ruby the temptations they'd already overcome. But had they really? Every look at Lula brought him a moment closer to the time she would be his. She would take his name and he would introduce her proudly as his bride, the most precious part of him. Her soft curl to his straight and narrow. Seeing her everyday back at the school, away from the cautious eye of her guardians, would bring all that back to the fore.

"Lula, your tuition is already paid. There is no way to get it back. Your sisters were already planning something special for when you graduated. They could certainly change those plans for a wedding if you both would like that. But should you desire to remain in school, in case something happens between you both before graduation and you *don't* wed, we support you."

Could that happen? Could anything take Lula from him? Of course, it could. He'd ruined so much with her that even now she hesitated. Lula reached up and pulled his string tie free of his neck. "This is mine until the day we are bound together as one. Then you may have it back. I will finish my classes because Ruby is right. She comes from a place of knowledge. You never know what might happen. If something were to happen to you, heaven forbid, I need a way to provide for myself."

Ruby let them go and backed away, gave Lula a quick nod, then turned and left the house, leaving them alone for the first time since they'd talked in the barn when they'd arrived. He took the tie and wrapped it twice around her wrist, tying it gently. "I love you, Lula Arnsby, and I never want another day of my life to pass without you in it."

Lula nodded back to him, staring at her wrist. "It won't be easy, probably the hardest thing we'll ever do."

He traced the line of her wrist up to the palm of her hand, then pulled her to him. "I know, but the reward will be a bit of heaven."

Chapter Twenty

He loved her. Lula hadn't been able to think of a single other thing since then. She'd burned the baked potatoes, scalded the coffee, and taken her nephew out for a walk in the snow...barefooted. All because the only one she could reasonably think of was Barton. In just a week, she'd have to return to the day in and day out of teaching school. She'd have to return to studying, and actually trying to complete her work, all with the constant thoughts of what life would be like when it was done. And those thoughts consumed her.

He'd done nothing but talk with her, hold her hand, brush his lips over her knuckles, and tell her he loved her. Every day was full of the things they shared together before they parted for the evening. But he wouldn't kiss her. He wanted to. She'd caught his glances to her lips in the evening as they sat on the couch in front of the fireplace. Her family had somehow managed to all find other things to do, even in the small space of the cabin Brody Ferguson let them use. Tonight, the whole family was up at the ranch house for the Christmas celebration. Lula and Barton had joined for the meal, then begged to leave.

Beau had given her a stern look, but trusted her. She prayed her trust was not misplaced. Knowing they could return any moment would keep both of them on their own end of the couch. At least she hoped. Now that her wedding appeared eminent, it seemed more important that they not touch. They were both aware it might lead down a path they shouldn't take.

After she'd been home for two days, she'd taken Hattie aside and asked her about the feelings that had seemed to drown out all her sense when Barton had kissed her. She'd begged for her silence in the matter. Hattie had told her that, not only was it normal to feel that temptation, it was good. Those wonderful feelings would grow with marriage, the closer she got to her husband, and through the sanctification of marriage. She'd explained how she'd worried over her own reaction to her dear Hugh. Though she'd never reacted to any other man like she did with Hugh, it was so powerful, she'd worried that he thought her brazen for wanting him.

Hattie's talk had put her mind at ease, but also made her want to wed Barton all the faster. Hattie had explained that feelings like that don't go away. They get stronger and time apart from the man you love only intensifies it. Marriage was the quickest way to get it under control. Hattie would know, she wed Hugh within two days of bringing him home.

At the house, Barton opened the door for her and let her inside. It was dark. He closed the door, keeping the chill at bay for a bit. He moved to tend to the banked fire, while she sat on the couch and waited for him. And soon, the rose glow of the fire poured soft light over the room. She did not move to light a lantern. It wasn't needed. He turned from his task and his soft eyes took in every inch of her.

She moved over for him to join her on the couch and he did, then held his arms open and she couldn't resist wrapping hers around him and letting him draw her close. He no longer looked like a teacher. He wore brown trousers much like her brothers-in-law, with a worn white shirt and brown vest. He'd been riding with Hugh and Beau to help them with ranch chores, as Aiden stayed close to the house. His wife, Jennie, was nearing her time, and everyone understood why he wouldn't want to be far out on the range when she could go into labor at any time with their second child.

"Merry Christmas, Lula," he whispered as he cradled her close. How she loved it when he just held her. No one had ever done such a thing for her.

She couldn't help the sigh that slipped from her lips. "Merry Christmas, Barton."

"Our next year might be quite different from this one. I wonder where we'll be?"

In her resolve to end her time at school, she'd forgotten all about the school Izzy had told her about that was allowing married teachers, but if she were going to finish...there was always a chance. "You never know, we could be teaching. There's a school that is taking married teachers."

He drew her away from him and looked her in the eye. "I thought you'd given up on teaching. Have I been replaced again so quickly?"

She rested her hand on his arm, hoping it would calm him. She hadn't mentioned it to anger him, only as a possibility.

"No, Barton. It would make no sense to start teaching when I could have to leave at any time. I see that now. I was merely saying that it is a possibility. We might even find a school where we might teach together. Can you imagine it, Barton? Working together?" The more she thought of it, the more perfect it sounded. She'd never have to spend another day alone. She could work with her dear husband to teach children until she was great with her own. Then she would stay at home and teach them.

Barton pulled her back into his arms. "Even if it's only a dream, it sounds like a wonderful one. I've never heard of a school doing such a thing. I was wondering what you thought about...ranching? My pa owns a very large spread in Belle Fourche. Even bigger than this one. I have brothers who will inherit first, but, I will get a portion. It would be enough to provide well for you your whole life."

A rancher's wife. That had never been a possibility before. He'd even told her he hadn't wanted to be a teacher, had only come to be with her. But he was so good at teaching. "I would follow you anywhere. But you *are* a good teacher. You should know that."

He drew his finger slowly up her arm, leaving little goosebumps on her skin, under her sleeve. As his finger trailed up her neck, she tipped her head, allowing him better access. It was without thought, as natural as the sunrise. She loved him, everything about him, including the way he made her heart race. He traced her jaw and tipped her head just so as his lips came down gently on hers. She'd waited all week for him. Her arms tightened around him, holding him close. His lips played gently over hers, refusing to spark the heated need as he'd done before.

It was a sweet caress of her lips.

He parted from her and tugged each pin loose from her hair. As it fell down her back, he brushed it with his fingers. "You are my dear one. If I've been given the gift to teach, then I will teach you how to love only me and I will teach our children how to be good and right. If I am a good teacher, then I will lead my family. I don't need a classroom to be a good teacher."

If he didn't, neither did she.

Lula's soft curls spilled over his hands as he cradled her head, trying to hold back from kissing her once again. She was a temptation to him. Just as potent as the whisper in his ear that it didn't matter, they would be married soon, was the quiet voice that sounded like his father, reminding him that it *did*. Until he stood before the Lord and made a covenant, Lula didn't belong to him and it wasn't right to take what wasn't his. Neither should he encourage her to give it, but that one decision was the most difficult one he'd made in his life.

Her lips were soft and darkened by kisses from moments before and he already wanted them again. They drew first his eyes, then his thoughts, and finally he succumbed, drawing nearer to her.

The front door swung open just as he brushed his lips against Lula's. Hattie growled and grabbed him, peeling Lula from his arms. "No! You can't do that!"

He'd only been holding her, what could've caused Hattie to get so angry? He glanced to Lula and realized what he'd done. With her hair undone and laying about her shoulders in sultry curls, he'd undressed her hair. He'd again taken liberties. Would he ever do right by this woman? *Lord, help me! She is too much of a temptation!*

Now that Lula was on the other end of the couch once again, Hattie drew a chair over. His arms already felt empty without her.

Hattie picked a few pins up from the floor and handed them to Lula. She was pink and wouldn't look at him as she twisted her hair and quickly shoved the pins in to hold it out of his reach again. When they were wed, he'd ask her to wear it down for him all the time. When Hattie cleared her throat, he realized he'd been staring.

"I'm sorry. You didn't catch what you thought you did." How could he say it was just her hair, it wasn't as if he'd tried anything else?

Hattie pegged him to his end of the couch with steely blue eyes. "Barton. If what all of my sisters have shared with me is true, every single one of us found out what a good kiss can do before we were wed. The one difference, every single one of us knew just when to stop. If you both can't, then you need to make sure you don't find yourselves alone. If that isn't possible, find a preacher. Paul says that it's better to be wed then to fight temptation, and it's true."

Hattie hung her blonde head and clasped her hands in front of her. "I come from the unique position of being the only one of the Arnsby sisters who wasn't a pure bride. I was forgiven, and in that sense, I was pure, but even if I'm forgiven, I'll never forget what I lived through. I cherish each moment with Hugh because he could've easily turned from me. I was not sweet nor chaste. I was a drunken prostitute, about the least appealing creature God could find, and yet, he rescued me."

He cast a quick glance at Lula before Barton leaned forward. "Hattie, I'm not trying to make a prostitute out of Lula…"

"In a way, you are. Every time your kiss tempts her away from the bride you want her to be, you push her closer to the act. Don't expect her to be able to stop if you can't. Fornication takes two, but you, Barton, are the man, the lead. We expect better of you. This is your chance to prove that you can lead your future wife and family."

That was what he wanted more than anything, and he'd convinced himself he was in the right because she was almost his. But almost wasn't close enough. He reached for Lula's hand. "I'm sorry. Can you forgive me? Can you walk beside me in this?" He'd always considered himself strong, but this was more than he could handle on his own.

Lula reached over, her wrist still held the tie he'd put on her days before. "The Lord will help both of us."

Hattie heaved a sigh. "Good. Now, what will you two do about this? Your break will be over soon. If you're getting married, we need to plan quickly."

Barton wanted to marry her, would've tossed her on his horse and rode into town that instant if Lula wanted it. But she slowly shook her head.

"I can't do that. My heart knows Barton will provide for me forever, but Ruby was right. I should finish my classes just in case something happens. If it's all right with Barton, we can get married right after graduation. I won't apply to be a student teacher. Barton will have his full certificate, and I will have the training done." She tipped her head down and pursed her lips as she waited for his response.

Barton drew her hand to his lips, but even that left him wanting more. "I will marry you when you ask, just don't make me wait too long. I'm not half as strong as I thought and I want you for my own."

Chapter Twenty-One

Lula fiddled with the black tie around her wrist, just under the cuff of her shirt as she waited for Izzy to come back from her Christmas holiday. The women's dormitory was steadily filling, both with girls coming back from break and their chatter. Izzy had told Lula she would be back the day before classes resumed, but it was getting quite close to sundown and she hadn't returned.

As Lula lit the lamp and did her best not to worry, Izzy finally arrived, but she didn't have luggage and only wore a coat, no muff or anything else that would suggest a long ride in a carriage.

"Lula! I have the most amazing news!" She held out her hand and a small gold band glistened back at her. "Harland surprised me by coming home with me. He'd already arranged it with my parents. For Christmas, he gave me the ring. We were married by a judge on our way here. We just couldn't wait. Harland is wiring my parents now and trying to secure an apartment for us in Spearfish so he can finish his year."

Lula searched her heart for the happiness she should feel, but only jealousy sat in the center of her thoughts. Izzy hadn't wanted to wed, she hadn't wanted to go with Harland at all.

"You...married? After all the things you said to me about future, and holding back because of dreams...you married...on a whim?"

Izzy's face crumpled. "I thought you, of all people, would understand. The attraction was just too great. When he surprised me, and we talked, it was just so perfect. Lula, I'm so sorry. You were right. I spoke out of a complete lack of knowledge. Harland and I hadn't even...well, I just didn't understand until now." Her cheeks bloomed pink.

Lula searched for the right words.

Forgiveness would be a start, but it was hard in coming.

"I'm just so shocked."

Izzy took her response as a welcome and fell right back into their old way of easy friendship. "Of course, you are! I am, so I'm not surprised that you are." She tossed her hat on the bed that used to be hers and dropped into the rocking chair with a contented sigh. "It's so wonderful, Lula." A secretive smile swept over Izzy's face. "All of it, it's just wonderful. And to think, I hadn't wanted to give Harland a chance at all. I'm so grateful to you, Lula. Look at me, prattling on. How was your break? What did you do?"

Practically gave myself to the teacher... Lula swept the thought from her head. She had to wait four more months to have the lovely ring on her own finger. She had to settle for Barton's tie for now.

"Barton came out to the ranch in Deadwood. He spoke to Beau and I think we'll be married in the fall."

Izzy frowned. "Why wait? I see no reason. You can be just like me. It isn't as if you'll teach if you're married. As a wife, you can help him and support him. Just think, you could grade papers for him, talk with him about the assignments everyone else has to do. You could even read the lectures and still learn, but there's no reason for you to sit there when your life companion is waiting! Don't make him wait!"

If only it were as easy for Barton as it was for another student. The students weren't under a contract. Barton would lose everything if he married her.

"We considered that, but it just wouldn't work. I'm here because I don't want to be away from him for the last four months of class and because he can't marry a student while he's under contract. We even considered, since he doesn't really want to be a teacher at all, of getting married once the professor comes back and just sacrificing the remainder of his year. Barton would do that for me, but I know he'd rather not. He is a man of his word and breaking one contract for another is wrong. I'm glad that you found Harland." She almost choked on her own anger. "I'm so glad that you've found happiness."

"No, you're not. I can see it in your eyes. I'm sorry I was so harsh with you before break. I shouldn't have been."

"So you've said. You were my only

Sparks in Spearfish

friend, the one I needed when I didn't understand, and you wouldn't listen to me. Now you want me to just accept that you've done what you told me not to do, and be happy for you? You can't just walk in here and wave your ring under my nose and not expect me to be hurt."

Izzy clutched her hands in front of her. "I know. I hope we can someday go back to being as we were."

"Will I still see you, or will you spend all your time in town?" Arguing about the past wouldn't do either of them any good. She'd gotten her point across and their friendship would probably always suffer for it.

"After I clean out my side of the room, I really will have no reason to be here. I already let the dean know that I would be dropping all of my classes. They returned the money for the days I have yet to take, which surprised me. I did leave my payment for this room. I didn't want you to have to pay for your own room when you weren't prepared to do so. Be careful, Lula. I didn't know before, but I know now how tempting love can be. If you need me, I'll be just down the hill. When I come back tomorrow to clean out my room, I'll tell you just where so you can visit me."

Izzy pulled her into a quick embrace. "Maybe I'll even let you invite your scoundrel so that you two can talk for a minute over tea." She giggled, and Lula couldn't help but join her. Picturing the young, rugged teacher with a delicate tea cup was absurd. "I'll plan for coffee." Izzy laughed as she swished out the door.

The holiday had been so full of people with her large family and Barton. Now, she was back at school, where she was surrounded by people, and more alone than ever.

Barton scoured the classroom for Lula. After spending hours with her every day for weeks, he missed even the sight of her. Professor Cook had met with him yesterday when they'd returned from the holiday, and he was well enough to take his job back, but assured Barton that he was now fully qualified to teach any class. Barton had been tempted to ask for his certificate right then. He could have swept Lula right from the campus and they could start their lives together.

Sparks in Spearfish

A faint hint of roses caught on the breeze and, though many women wore the fragrance, none quite like Lula. She sat behind him and he turned to take her in.

"Good morning, Mr. Oleson." She kept her voice down, her face impassive, but she could never tame her eyes.

"Good morning, Miss Arnsby. Where is your friend Izzy? It's rare to see you two apart."

Harland chose that moment to walk in, talking loudly about his holiday exploits to the other men.

Heat crept up Lula's face as mention of her closest friend came up in conversation that had no business in a teaching classroom. Though Izzy was no longer qualified to be a teacher, her new husband had no such issues. Barton cleared his throat. "Mr. Lawson, would you stay after class for a moment, please?"

Tension coiled between the two, a test of wills between two men the same age, neither of whom respected the other. "Yes...sir." Harland gave a smug smile and sat heavily in his seat, his few friends sitting nearby and continuing their conversation in lower tones.

Lula hung her head. "Izzy would

be mortified. She was so happy to be married. Why would he do that?"

Lula wiped a tear from her eye and he wanted to throttle Harland. Instead, he drew his kerchief from his pocket and handed it to Lula. As she reached for it, his tie, bound to her wrist fortified him. She was waiting for him, ready to be with him and him alone. And he would never degrade her in such a way.

Professor Cook strode into the classroom, with only a slight limp that told of his time away. "Good morning, class." His strident voice was far from welcoming. "You've been doing quite well in my absence, but let's finish this year strong, knowing your futures aren't far away. I have, in fact, three letters in my desk requesting teaching assistants for next year and I will only give those to the most outstanding in my class. The rest will have to find your own." His gaze swept the room and landed on Lula, then slowly rested on Barton. "We are one short from where we started, that increases your odds."

Was that a challenge? Would the professor try to get his students to reduce the size of the class just for teaching referrals? What if he chose Lula? Would she want to go or would

Sparks in Spearfish

she still want to stay with him? His heart should trust her. But until he put a real ring on her finger, doubt remained.

The day lingered long, the evening shadows finally forcing the professor to accept that class needed to end. Barton turned in his seat to bid Lula to stay, but she was already most of the way out of the door. He glanced to Harland and notched his head toward the professor. Harland squinted at him for a moment, then a slow smile spread over his face. Dread rose to the back of Barton's throat in the form of bile.

Professor Cook waited at his desk and Barton came to the front. This was the part of teaching he hated. Confrontation on a ranch was settled much differently than in a classroom, and the only time he'd ever been forced to deal with anything like it was in class when another boy had started picking on Lula. He'd done it once, and never again. His pa had never encouraged fighting, but with three older brothers, he learned quick how to defend himself. Defending Lula had come as second nature.

Harland smiled as he waited by the desk, but Barton spoke up first. "Sir, Mr. Lawson was having a rather inappropriate and loud conversation before class started. He showed very little tact and some of the young ladies in class heard it."

"You mean your precious Lula heard it, don't you, Mr. Oleson?"

Professor Cook glanced between the two. "Mr. Lawson, keep your private talks, private. Parents will have you out on the street if you aren't careful. You have a promising career ahead of you if you can learn when to speak and when to shut your mouth. Dismissed."

Harland nodded and narrowed his eyes at Barton as he left the room. The professor turned his gaze on Barton. "Don't try to defend yourself, I know exactly what he was alluding to. I could see it on the very first day of class. What are your intentions, Barton?"

His stomach turned to rock, but what did he have to lose if the professor already knew? "I intend to marry her."

"Now or later?" Professor Cook rested his hands on his desk, folding them.

"After graduation." Why would it matter? If his professor knew, his time as an assistant was over.

"Good. I also had my eye on Miss

Sparks in Spearfish

Arnsby in a completely separate fashion. There is a very small country school in Belle Fourche, perhaps you've heard of it? The school is just west of Belle Fourche with only twenty students. I think she would make an excellent teacher there. I was planning to recommend her."

No. If she got one of the few recommendations... She might never pick him. She could be on her own, why would she need him? "Sir, why did you ask what my plans were, if you were going to take away my chances?" He backed into the nearest desk and sat.

"I asked because that particular school has been in need for over a year. They won't care if their teacher is married, and they will love that her husband is from the area. It would make it even easier to accept her, don't you think so?"

"So, I don't have to wait? We could marry right away?" He had to find Lula to tell her.

"No, I'm afraid not. You still have your contract. If you're caught with Miss Arnsby, it will ruin your contract and will destroy her chances of graduating and getting this referral. You've waited this long, just keep up the wait for another few months, knowing that the Lord sees your plight and is making a way for you."

Now, he just had to bide his time and stay away from Lula so that the Lord's plan could actually come to fruition.

Chapter Twenty-Two

Her room was too quiet. Lula drummed her fingers over her desk. Barton would never treat her as Harland had treated Izzy, would he? He'd never speak flippantly in front of a group about their intimacies... Izzy would be there to collect her belongings any moment, but would she be alone, or would Harland be there to help her? A sick dread lodged in her throat. She should tell Izzy, but how?

A short rap on the door tugged her thoughts back and Lula stood to answer as Izzy opened it and peeked inside. "Lula! Oh, how I miss you! I scoured the whole apartment this morning and got the few things we have settled, but then it was just terribly boring."

Izzy drew Lula over to the bed she used to occupy and sat her down. "Harland was in the strangest mood when he came home from class today. I told him I was going to see you and he became rather angry."

Lula worried her lip. If she were in Izzy's position, she would want to know to confront Barton, but Harland was different and he and Izzy had only spent a handful of evenings together.

"Lula?" Izzy tilted her head to look her straight in the eye and the secret lodged in her throat. Izzy would be crushed to know that Harland wasn't happy.

"Harland was probably embarrassed. He got into a bit of hot water in class today." She wouldn't say anything more. If Izzy asked her husband, he could tell her.

"Harland? He's so quiet and reserved. I can't imagine him ever being over-boisterous. Perhaps it was just coming back to class after such a lovely holiday."

If Harland's words were true, the holiday had not been quite what he was hoping for. Harland had discovered that women wore garments that changed their shape, and Izzy was no different from any other woman, and Izzy was more rounded than most. He'd felt cheated to find that she didn't look anything like the silhouette of her skirts. Hopefully, he would be pleased with the woman he chose, in time.

Izzy laid her hand on Lula's arm as she prattled on about Harland. She'd have to sit and listen about the man forever now. "Oh, and Lula, I've got everything ready for your visit. Friday evening, I'm going to invite you and Mr. Oleson for supper. There's no reason you can't because it would be me setting it up, not you. If anyone would ask, I would say that I'd invited my dearest friend and Harland invited Barton. It was purely happenstance that you ended up at our home together, next to each other at our table. And if Harland knows what's good for him, he best not say a word."

Though it had only been a little over one day since she'd sat at a table with Barton, it was something to look forward to, something to give her hope to make it through the week. Without that, there was nothing. Her schooling no longer held her attention, since she'd probably never use it. Above all, she wanted Barton.

"That sounds wonderful, thank you so much Izzy. Thank you for understanding."

Izzy gave her a wicked smile. "I may not have known my Harland long before he proposed, but I know him well now. You and Barton have been acquainted so much longer, and I see the need between you. Now that I've felt it, I can't even fathom what you're going through. I'm afraid I missed my dear Harland so much during the day that I almost threw myself at him when he returned home. He may have even bit a little put off by my brazen behavior." Izzy's cheeks flushed and she laughed as her glance flitted over the room.

"I keep telling myself that the Lord created these passions in us for our husbands... But when you are taught your whole life to be chaste and modest... Perhaps, I merely went too far and my poor, quiet Harland just wasn't prepared for such a bride."

He hadn't been prepared for any bride at all. Lula couldn't imagine Barton ever turning away any affection unless they were in a position to be seen by others. He'd always drawn her to him, cherished her. Hattie had taken her aside during the holiday break and explained just what happened between men and women once they were wed, and how powerful the urges could be, but Lula had never actually experienced those feelings. She had no business passing on information that would only be second hand, yet...if it were her in Izzy's position, she would want to know.

"I don't think there's anything wrong with having passion for your husband. The Lord created love. He *is* love, and it was His plan that this type of love be shared only between a married couple, but..." Lula sighed and bit her lip for a moment. What could be done? It wasn't like Izzy could leave him, but she had to know.

"Izzy. I'm sorry. It wasn't that Harland was overexcited in class today. He was taken to task for saying some horrible things...intimate things...as he came into class today. I didn't want to say anything, it was so embarrassing, but you have to know."

Izzy froze. "He talked about our intimacies...in class?" Izzy turned pale, then red as a radish. "Did everyone hear?"

She couldn't say that, but she and Barton had heard, and obviously the three other men Harland was speaking to. "I don't know. He wasn't yelling, but he wasn't being particularly quiet, either." Lula felt her own face flame, remembering his mention of certain curves on Izzy, how some were inadequate and others, far too much for his taste.

Izzy was silent for a moment, then pursed her lips. "Well, it isn't like I'll be sitting in that class anymore, so I won't have to suffer the embarrassment of seeing those people."

Her hands shook and she clutched her gloves. Her chin hardened and the stubborn Izzy, the only girl out of eight children, appeared before her.

"I understood the desires he was talking about, because, I had to know. I had to talk to my sister while I was home...to make sure I wasn't as horrible and...fallen...as I felt." Lula clutched her handkerchief at the ready.

Izzy avoided Lula's eyes. "I see you finally talked to Hattie about her past. You've held her at a different standard than your other sisters for quite some time. Have you now forgiven her?" Izzy's voice was quiet, probing. Had she been unforgiving with Hattie? It had been difficult to understand what had happened. She'd only been twelve when Hattie left, or rather, was taken. She knew now that Hattie had been tricked into leaving, then sold into prostitution. But for so long there had been a heaviness over their whole house. Hattie had come back completely changed, forgiven and free of her guilt...and in love.

"I guess I didn't realize I hadn't, but yes. Hattie and I talked about my future, Barton, and what having a good marriage means. She's always been frank and I needed that, because I could never ask any of my other sisters..." *about the passion Barton had stirred*. Why was it so hard to admit it out loud? Even when Izzy had made a similar declaration?

"I'm glad. You've always spoken about how wonderful your friendships are with your sisters, and I'd always been curious about what held you back from Hattie. I've only met her the once when she and her husband came with Mr. Rockford to pick you up."

A harsh knock on the door had Lula scrambling to answer it. Too many questions about Hattie would only lead to opening Hattie's old secrets back up. Those were fine just where they were, in the past. Lula opened the door and the house mother stood with her hands on her hips and a glare like no other. The long hair that stuck out just above her lip was quivering.

"Lula Arnsby, there is a man waiting downstairs for his wife. He is rather impatient that she hurry."

Izzy stood and covered her mouth with her fingertips. "Oh my! I haven't packed a single thing! I've been sitting here chatting. What will he think? He's been sitting down there waiting for me. Poor dear."

Poor dear, my foot. Though, even Izzy's endearment didn't sound quite as besotted as it had when she'd first arrived. Lula swallowed the retort. She said a prayer that Izzy and Harland were able to work out their differences. "I'll save you the trouble. I'll ask Mr. Oleson to rent a buckboard from the livery in Spearfish and we can bring the rest of your things on Friday, then we can just walk back to campus after supper."

"Oh, Lula, you would do that? Thank you so much! I do hate to keep him waiting any longer."

"Of course, I would. Go." She

shooed her friend from the room and closed the door. It marked a change in her friendship. No more could she say that Izzy was her closest and dearest friend. She was married to a man who didn't love her, at least not yet, and she would hesitate to share anything with her for fear she might tell Harland. Close and dear friends didn't lie or keep secrets. Harland's thoughtless words and her own crippling inability to speak would change the friendship. It might never be repaired.

A note with scrawling pen lay on Barton's desk in the teachers' office. His hope soared. He hadn't spoken to Lula after class, since she'd dashed away, and he hadn't seen her at supper, either. His eyes craved just one sight of her. His ears, one word.

He picked up the note and almost tossed it back, it wasn't her writing. He'd know it anywhere. Though most women wrote similarly, with penmanship being one thing teachers pounded into their students, Lula's writing was somehow different. He'd recognize it anywhere.

Lula's name at the bottom caught his eye and he picked up the note, scanning it quickly. Izzy Lawson wanted him to come for a visit and Lula was to be there. He set the note in the burn pile so it wouldn't be found. Harland would never let that opportunity pass. He would find a way to put he and Lula in a compromising situation. It wouldn't be good to go, no matter how much he wanted to spend time with Lula. Not with Harland there.

Barton grabbed his hat and slid the bill of the almost new Stetson through his hands. His pa had gotten him the hat when he'd graduated, hoping Barton would change his mind and stay with the family business. It hadn't happened, but he still missed the ranch, the work, even his brothers. Having Lula there would make it perfect. Even if she were working, she would be there making his life complete.

He slid the hat on as he ducked out the door and headed down the hill for a ride. He'd made it to the edge of the campus, near the last lamppost, when he spotted Lula walking ahead. He jogged toward her and she startled and turned just as he approached. Her look of utter happiness stopped his heart. "Hello, beautiful." The words slipped from him before he could think.

Her cheeks glowed under his words and he reached for her. She met him and they embraced for a moment. Would it ever stop being a wonder how well she fit just right to him?

Lula stepped back and her gaze slid down to his feet. "I'm sorry I rushed out of class this evening. Izzy was going to stop by and I didn't want to miss her."

There was more to it, Lula was keeping something from him. She never avoided his eyes, not anymore. "And did you see her?"

"Yes, she had a wonderful idea, she was going to invite you and I to her home on Friday so we could spend a few minutes together." She reached for his hand and he couldn't keep from giving her what she desired. It was his biggest problem and greatest weakness.

"I'm sorry, Lula. I won't be able to go..."

Her gaze flew back to his and the hurt took his breath from his lungs.

"Why not? Don't you want to see me outside of school? It was perfect, because they are married and Harland could've invited you, don't you see?"

He could see, but she didn't. She hadn't been in the classroom when Harland had chatted with the professor.

"Harland wants to get you expelled and me fired. I doubt Izzy asked Harland first, and if she did, and he accepted, it was so that he'd have an excellent excuse to report us. As it is, the professor already knows."

"He knows?" Her voice squeaked and she stepped away from him. He wanted to pull her right back against him, to cradle her fear away.

"Then all is lost..." She took two steps farther away from him. "If he knows, it's only a matter of time until I'm expelled and then I won't be able to see you for months."

Barton reached for her. "No, Lula. It's not like that, let me explain."

"I shouldn't be seen out here with you. Anyone could walk down the hill. I'm so sorry Barton. I'll go on Friday, but I understand why you won't be. I'll be careful around Harland."

"Lula, would you just wait?" If he yelled, he'd draw the attention of others, exactly what he didn't want to do, but he couldn't have her afraid. He reached for her again and she dashed into his arms, throwing her arms around his neck and her lips to his. He couldn't breathe, couldn't think. Her kiss was need in every sense, her fear pouring through her and into him. He stroked her hair and tried to slow her down.

As she pulled from him, a tear streaked down her cheek. "I'm so sorry, but I couldn't just leave you. I love you, Barton." She bunched her skirt in her fists and ran back toward the school, leaving him.

How could he get her to understand that she wasn't in danger from the professor, only the dean, and Harland? Though, if she was afraid to be seen with him at all, they would be safe, her future secure. But the burn of her lips on his proved how hard that was going to be.

Chapter Twenty-Three

Lula tucked her muff into her coat and buttoned it tight. She had to rush to the livery, rent a wagon, bring it back, load all of Izzy's belongings, and drive it down to Izzy's new home in town, all before it got too dark. Thank heavens she'd had all week to pack Izzy's trunk and she'd sent a note to Barton to have him haul the full trunk to the wagon. Harland would have to carry it up to their apartment, since Barton wouldn't be joining them.

Having Barton in her room was terrifying, so she'd told the house mother what needed to happen and that he would need to find the room.

The old hen had no trouble telling Lula to stay far away, she would be nowhere near her room when Barton was there. She'd better be waiting by the rig.

The January wind bit at her cheeks. She'd hoped for warmer weather, but in the hills, chilly was preferable to snowy. She'd sent a note down to the livery the day before to have a rig ready for her and she'd promised an advance with a little money from Christmas. As she ducked into the warm livery to pay, a familiar face waited for her near the front.

"Barton? What are you doing here?" Her heart skipped a beat. Outside of class, dressed in work clothes for riding, he was handsome enough to take her breath away.

"I just got back from a quick ride after class, and thought I'd help you while I was here." He stepped toward her and then directed her back out into the cold.

"Wait! I still need to pay for it." She twisted to return in and Barton caught her before she fell.

"I took care of it. I know you don't have much right now. You aren't working and there's no real need for your family to send you money while you're at school. Since I'm working, would you let me do this for you?"

He had an old-fashioned way, chivalrous, that made her see he was doing everything for her, but also made her enjoy it. "I'll concede to your help, Mr. Oleson. Thank you." She held out her hand like a regal lady, since that's how he made her feel. He tucked his gloved hand under hers and drew it to his lips for a bare second.

They hadn't hitched a buckboard for her, but more of a light buggy with just enough room in the back for Izzy's trunk. Barton held her hand until they reached the rig and he helped her up to the seat, then came around the back and climbed in next to her.

His smile warmed her right down to her toes. "Have you ever driven one of these? Can I trust you to get it back to the livery in one piece?" he teased.

She swatted his shoulder. "Yes, I've lived on a ranch for years. Beau showed me how to drive before he'd even let me ride."

Barton picked up the lines and gave them a flick. The horse made quick work of the short drive and soon she was right back at the women's dormitory. Barton rushed inside and reappeared shortly heaving the massive trunk, Mrs. Maddox, the house mother, on his heels.

He shoved it in the back and laughed as he came back around to her side. He rested his hand against hers where she held onto the seat.

"I wish I felt comfortable enough to come with you, but I have to think about our future. I don't want you to miss having a good time with Izzy because you were too worried about Harland seeing something between us."

"And you're sure there's no worry from the professor?" He'd caught up with her after class and explained that her fear was unwarranted. She'd been afraid to even enter the classroom.

"The professor will only act if he's forced to. He has to think about his job, as well. I shouldn't linger here. People will wonder why. I'll see you tomorrow." He backed away from the rig and waved, then turned and walked away.

If she didn't rush, it would be dark before she made it down the hill. She flicked the lines, prodding the horse to speed up. Harland and Izzy now lived above the office of a real estate lawyer. It would be easy to find right on the main street of Spearfish.

The wide streets were easy to navigate in the twilight with very few people dashing about. Most were in their warm homes eating and enjoying time with their families. Harland waited for her outside the real estate office, blowing on his hands and shuffling back and forth.

"I was beginning to think you weren't coming. What took you so long? Too many goodbyes for Mr. Oleson?" His mouth tipped in a sneer.

What had her friend found likable in Harland? Though, he hadn't acted that way prior to marrying Izzy. He'd seemed quiet and reserved.

"No, Mr. Lawson, I was bringing Izzy's trunk and we only got out of class at a quarter past, as you know." She climbed down and waited for him to offer to take the rig back to the livery.

He turned to the task and then called for her, "Open that door, there on the right. We'll be ready for you as soon as you get back."

Lula gasped. Barton had gone out of his way to help her, to pay for it, to drive the rig back, to carry the huge trunk. Harland couldn't even be civil. The comparison was stark. What would being married to this man do to her beloved Izzy? Lula closed the door behind Harland and climbed back up into the rig. The livery was only a few blocks away, at least she wouldn't have to walk far in the dark. She flicked the lines and set the horse toward its home.

Leaving the livery, the streets of Spearfish were dim. The moon was blanketed in clouds and every shadow seemed murkier than the last. Though it wasn't terribly late, the darkness bore down on her. Spearfish was a wealthier town, with farmers, cattlemen, and business owners. It was like night and day compared to her Deadwood home. Whereas Deadwood had a whole separate night life that was loud and bright, Spearfish slumbered after nightfall.

A man strode toward her and she shivered. The door to the Lawson's apartment was still a block away. If the man didn't turn his steps, she'd have to walk right by him.

"Lula Arnsby?" The man called from about a block away.

Her heart raced and she stopped, clutching the wall next to her. "Yes, who's there?"

"Amos, from school. Harland asked me to join you tonight."

Why would Izzy agree to such a thing when she knew Lula only wanted to be with Barton? Neither of them liked Amos very much. She hesitated, unsure of what to say. "I didn't realize anyone else would be coming."

Amos started toward her and stopped a few steps away. He hadn't been there when Harland had been speaking about Izzy, because he wasn't a teaching student, but she suspected he knew just the same. "Harland tells me that you've decided you don't want to teach anymore. Why are you still coming to class, if you don't mind me asking? Seems to me it's taking time away from the rest of the class if you're just there for sport."

Bile rose in the back of her throat, what sort of rumors was Harland spreading and where would he hear such a thing? The only answer was his wife, who wouldn't see any issue with telling her husband everything.

"I don't know where you hear your stories, but they aren't true." She made to push past him, but he grabbed her wrist and whipped her around to face him once again.

Sparks in Spearfish

"You forget, my closest friend has sat in that class all year long. We all know there's more going on between you and the teacher than you want anyone to know about. If you're going to be a loose skirt, there's plenty of us who could use a little attention. You don't have to save it all for the teacher. Though, I bet he gives you some pretty good grades as payment. How many kisses for an A?" Amos swiped his arm under his nose.

Her stomach roiled and her hands shook. How dare he accuse her of such things and what could she do to stop him. Before he could finish a step toward her, she slapped him. Her leather riding gloves making a satisfying smack across the fleshy part of his cheek. He groped for her other wrist and she kicked at him to get away. Her heart clamored against her stays as she fought for freedom.

A gunshot pierced the night and Amos dropped her wrists and shrank back against the building. Barton appeared out of the shadows, a pistol pointed in the air resting in his right hand. Her cavalry had arrived. "I suggest you make your way to wherever you were headed Amos." Barton's teacher voice brooked no argument, and the gun backed it up. He offered her his hand and she tucked herself into his side. Safe.

"You think you can keep this away from the administration, Oleson? You've just earned yourself a report. I saw you out here, alone, with Lula, walking arm in arm down the streets of Spearfish, and now, because of your gunshot, others will see you too. Say goodbye to your teaching career." He shoved past Barton and strode toward Harland and Izzy's door.

Barton holstered his gun and then wrapped both arms around her. "I couldn't just let you face them alone. I'd changed my mind and planned to stop by and offer to take you home if things weren't going well. I'm so glad I did." He rubbed his stubbled chin over her head and she clung to him, letting him absorb the fear. "Walk with me?"

She nodded, still unable to speak. He didn't let her go, just held her close to his side as they walked back toward the school. She'd have to send Izzy a note in the morning and let her know why she'd never made it to supper, but she couldn't leave Barton and didn't want to face Harland or Amos any more.

Lula cleared her throat and glanced up at him. "We'll need to do something. They will report this in the morning and you'll lose your position. Our plans have to change. We'll have to think of something new. If you think they would let you stay, I'll go home and we can write letters until the end of term."

"I love that you're willing to sacrifice your dream of teaching for me, but it seems foolish to do that. You were the one who wanted to teach, Lula, not me. If anyone should go home and write letters, it should be me. Perhaps it's what I should've done to begin with. Instead of forcing myself back into your life, I could have written to you, begging you to forgive a little boy who just wanted some attention from his girl."

Lula stopped them and wrapped both arms around his waist. "Barton, you're forgiven. I'm so sorry for the hateful words I said to you. I didn't understand, wasn't ready to understand, what you were doing."

"I'm so sorry for the things I did to you. I wish I could take back every last tear I caused. I just wanted you to notice me. I wanted to feel your soft hair running through my fingers. I'd never seen a girl as pretty as you. And now you're a woman and I don't think the Lord made angels any lovelier."

Welcome heat burned up her cheeks. "You're too much, Barton Oleson."

He leaned down and kissed her gently just under each eye. "Hopefully, I'm just enough for you, Lula Arnsby. Will you marry me when you graduate?"

His soft wool coat brushed against her cheek as she embraced him close. "Yes, I will. I wish I could tonight."

"So do I, my buttercup. So do I."

Chapter Twenty-Four

The small hard chair outside the dean's office had never felt quite so uncomfortable. Lula sat next to him, her leg bouncing with her nerves. He'd already assured her, three times, that he was more than willing to offer to leave if they would just let her stay, but he didn't want to leave. Not really. She wasn't supposed to be apart from him, he could feel it down to his angry heart. He should let it go, he and Lula were in the wrong, they hadn't been following the rules set by the school, but they also hadn't hurt anyone else.

As the dean's secretary opened the wooden door to the dean's office,

Barton rose to his feet and offered Lula a hand. Best to show the utmost respect if he hoped to convince the dean to allow Lula to stay. Professor Cook exited the dean's office and smiled, thanked the secretary, and then indicated they should follow him to his desk.

Barton followed Lula and the Professor and sat on the opposite side of his desk.

"Mr. Oleson, Miss Arnsby." He nodded to each of them as he sat down. "I was grateful that you came to me right away this morning before any of this was reported. That gave me a chance to head off the problem with the dean. He was not pleased by it, but he's also a married man who understands that sometimes you don't choose who you love. The Lord can pick the most unlikely of people to put together. For instance, when you, Barton, arrived back at school just a few days after leaving last summer and requested to take the teacher course for the purpose of doing your apprenticeship with us for this year... I was curious. I looked up your file, which, interestingly, was chock full of history with one particular girl." He turned to Lula and regarded her for a moment. "That intrigued me, but I kept it to myself. You were an excellent student. I've never seen better, but the moment I saw you speaking to Miss Arnsby that very first day, I knew. You weren't in my classroom to teach. That was never your intent."

His professor had seen right through him the whole time. They'd hidden for nothing. "I'm sorry, sir."

"No need to apologize. My wife found it particularly romantic, but she has that bent about her. Now, we have a problem. Any time you both are together, there will be suspicion. So, here is my solution. You may take mine, or you can do as you suggested and forfeit your contract."

The contract didn't matter anymore. Ranching didn't have his heart, neither did teaching. He just needed some job to care for Lula, to provide for her and hopefully his family. "I'm listening, sir."

"If I were to transfer your apprenticeship to the primary school for the remaining three months, you and Lula could marry if you wish. Though, I must caution you." He took Lula's hands and pressed them for a moment, then laid them down. "Lula, there is a school in Belle Fourche looking for a teacher. They've been waiting so long, they can most likely be convinced to take a married teacher. However, if they should be unhappy... You risk never working again."

Barton reached for her hand and wove her fingers within his. Whatever she chose would determine their life. Every choice he'd made for almost a year had been to woo this one woman to his side. All so that she would choose to stay by him.

Lula dipped her head and he squeezed her hand. How she hated to be the center of attention, and he wished she didn't have to be, but she had to make this choice. She cast him a weak smile, but at least she understood.

"Barton, if you're willing to remain here with the younger students, I don't want you to go." She turned back to the professor and took a long breath and let it out slowly. "Sir, I'd like to finish and try for the teaching job. If they don't like me or they decide that having a married teacher isn't working, then I'll be a wife." She clasped his hand tightly. "It is also a noble profession." His heart was fit to burst. She'd been so opposed to *just* being his wife, of being the sole reason he worked, that he'd felt like

Sparks in Spearfish

less of a man for even offering it to her. Her desire to fill the role of his wife renewed his faith in himself.

The professor nodded slowly. "I can do that and I think you're right, Miss Arnsby. And if you're blessed with children, your teaching will not stop. It will be continuous, *train them up in the way that they should go.*"

Barton pushed to his feet and drew Lula along with him. "So, now the only question is, do we marry now, or wait until the end of the year?" If they'd been anywhere but in his professor's office, he'd have gotten down on his knees and begged her. He was through with hiding and acting as if what he felt for Lula was wrong.

She reached up and cupped his cheek. Her smile amazed him. "All of my sisters, save one, were married on very short notice. I think they are used to it by now."

His arms wrapped around her waist of their own accord and he kissed her soundly, with the professor chuckling in the background. When he separated from her, she blushed deeply and he covered her warm cheeks with his palms. "Thank you, Lula. For giving me another chance."

A laugh bubbled from her. "I must be the most foolish woman alive to not only offer, but to want to have your children, Barton. I hope they don't show me love the same way you did when you were a boy."

If only he'd talked to his mother about Lula back then. But now, his ma would be so proud and he couldn't wait for them to meet. "I've never treated my mother with anything other than love and respect, and I'll guide any children we have in exactly how it should be done."

The professor cleared his throat. "Might I suggest we send a few telegrams?"

Did he want to wait for his family to come or should he just tell them he'd married? Hadn't he just said he'd never disrespected his mother? She would be so disappointed.

"Tell them the wedding will be Friday. That should give everyone enough time to get here."

Lula wrapped both arms around him as they left the professor's office. Holding her in the open was glorious. He didn't have to watch for anyone. Harland sat outside the dean's office in the chair Barton had been in before. He rushed to his feet as his jaw dropped open.

Sparks in Spearfish

"What's the meaning of this?" He gestured at them. "You're so brazen now about breaking the rules that you can't even help yourselves in the full light of day?"

Barton flexed his hand. If his brother had been so flippant, it would've led to an argument. Lula pressed her head to his chest.

"We are simply excited, Mr. Lawson. Barton and I are to be married." She raised her head and stared at Harland. "You would understand about that excitement, wouldn't you?"

Was she testing Harland? They both knew he wasn't happy. Her threat would carry weight if Harland took it seriously. His father had always said, happy wife, happy life. You don't want the woman who cooks for you to be angry. A hungry man is a desperate one.

Harland sat back down in the chair with a heavy thump and mumbled, "Yes, I suppose I would."

"Good day, Mr. Lawson. Please give my best to your wife and let her know that I am to be married on Friday. I would love for *her* to attend."

Barton gave Harland a nod, it was all he could manage. His Lula smoothed over the rough spots in him already. He helped her with her coat from the cloak hall by the doors and they stepped out into the sunlight. He turned her to face him, this was where he had to start guiding her, protecting her. Even from himself. "Lula, it would be too easy for me to ask more of you than I ought, knowing you will be mine forever in less than a week. Would you join me for every meal, and not let ourselves be caught alone, until after we've said our vows?"

The campus was empty on a Saturday morning, they were the only souls walking. Lula stretched up on her toes and brushed her lips gently against his, quickly moving back to her spot tucked under his arm. "I look forward to the time when I never have to leave your side again."

Chapter Twenty-Five

Lula's family arrived on Thursday, along with Barton's, and her heart was full as all the women embraced as they met. The men formed a wide circle and talked quietly. Ruby brought one trunk with them. Inside it, along with the clothes for all her sisters, was her wedding dress. The same one Frances had worn a few years before, with a tiered white lace skirt and a bodice, with an elegant pleated sweep down the front so it would appear the woman that wore it was tiny. Lula didn't care, Barton had held her in his arms. He knew how small she really was.

Nervousness crept up her spine as she thought about the dress...and after. Her moment with Barton behind the bush had been so long ago, and since the holiday break, they had been so diligent. But would he look on her with disgust as Harland had with Izzy? Her dear friend had been fooled into thinking he was just as happy as she was, would Barton be the same? He'd made so many changes for her, would he regard her as a bother if she didn't meet his expectations—and how could she? She had no experience, whatsoever.

Barton met her gaze and his eyes narrowed. He clapped Beau on the shoulder and said something, then made his way toward her through the large clutch of mingling family. He drew her to the side and ran a gentle hand down her arm, holding her. "What's bothering you? Our family is here for our wedding and you looked like you wanted to hide under the wagon."

She hadn't thought of that. If it would've helped, she might. Perhaps Hattie would give her one more lesson, or would Barton think *less* of her for knowing? If she were a child again, she would stomp her foot. There was no right answer and she'd never met a problem that didn't have one.

He tipped his head and rested his broad forehead against hers. "Let me in, Lula. I can't take away your fears if you don't. If you tell me, at least we can face it together."

In less than a day, she would be partnered for life with this wonderful man, yet telling him such fears mortified her. "I'm nervous about tomorrow." That was truth, she'd spent all week memorizing her vows and doing her school work. How her sisters and Izzy had managed it at the drop of a hat, she couldn't fathom. It had taken her days.

He smiled, his eyes so close to hers. She was wrapped in his warmth. "I'm nervous, too. What if I don't make you happy? What if I don't please you? You are all that is soft and good, and I am rough. I know that when I hold you in my arms, you fit perfectly. Like water in a pitcher, you meld to me. I know you're worried about what Harland said. He doesn't love her. He doesn't wake up every morning and choose to kiss his wife and thank the Lord for what he has. For those who have been given much, much is expected. I have been given much and you can expect that

I will be thankful for every moment, good or bad."

He made her want to cling to him and every word. He'd ridden out to meet his family and the scent of leather that was always subtly with him, was strong and she breathed it in. She'd never tire of it. Barton wove his fingers into her nape and left a kiss on her forehead. "I don't want to leave you, but my father and brothers are going to help me move everything into our apartment. It's only temporary since we'll be leaving at the end of term. They didn't bring much, but it should be enough to start a home."

Home. "We already have all we need to start a home. Go. I'll be waiting here for you tomorrow." And all the rest of her life.

He was as nervous as a horse in a river. Barton dressed in his best suit, then his pa had driven him to the small white church on the edge of Spearfish. And now he waited. Lula and her family hadn't arrived yet. Izzy had come, but Harland had not, of course. Lula hadn't told him he was invited.

Where could she be?

He paced to the end of the aisle and back to the front of the church again. His mother stopped him as he reached the back of the church and led him to the pew. "Sit, my nervous boy."

He sighed and obeyed, scraping his clammy hands down the front of his pants. Nothing short of 'she's waiting outside' was going to calm him down.

"She will be here. It takes a woman a while to get ready on her wedding day. She has more to prepare than just her clothes."

He glanced to his ma then up to the wooden cross hanging in front of the church. "What else would she have to get ready? Does she have to make up her mind again?"

"In a way, yes. Just as you should. Today, you will enter into a covenant. In your excitement, I hope you remembered that. It's one of the few things the Lord asks us to join and it *should not ever* be broken. Not in this life, anyway."

"I don't ever want it to break." And that was the truth. His life was an empty shell without Lula.

Ma patted his leg. "I know. It's easy to say that on your wedding day when you're looking at life through the lens of hope, but there will come a day when you must choose to love Lula, just as there will come a day when she will have to choose to love you. You'll have left your socks on the end of the bed one too many times and she will want to put castor oil in your soup."

His Lula? He couldn't even picture it. Even when she'd hated him, she'd only used words to cut him.

"Be good to one another, give each other grace. Love deeply, because sometimes the Lord *does* take away, but be there to fill in the holes that those losses leave behind."

Lula stepped across the threshold, a white gauzy veil covering her face and melding with the flowing white of her dress. She truly was an angel, a pure bride just for him, because they'd done what was right.

His mother stood and gripped his shoulder for just a moment then turned to Lula. "You're lovely, dear. I'll go get the minister."

He couldn't breathe or speak; how could this vision be his? She was waiting for him and reached both hands out for him. He couldn't deny her.

His feet were sluggish and he felt like an oaf compared to her elegance. "She's right, you're more than lovely."

Lula's head dipped for a moment and a nervous laugh quivered from under the veil. "I don't know how you can tell that, I'm behind all this fabric, you can't even see me, but I was told that's how they do this now. Hattie never had to wear one."

He'd been told of Hattie's past, that she and Ruby were the only two who hadn't worn white on their wedding days. Hattie because her dress had been made for her, and Ruby because she was on the way to rescue her sisters when she wed Beau.

"I know what your face looks like, I've pictured it in my mind's eye for so long. Can you believe we're finally here?"

She shook her head but the long veil hardly moved. "This week has seemed like a year."

And it had. Every night, as he'd left her after supper, it had been harder and harder to say goodbye.

The minister strode in and laid a hand on each of them. "Are you ready? Everyone is here."

He sent Lula out the back and led

Barton to stand in the front. The minister's wife went to the organ and began to play as his brothers and parents came in, then Lula's sisters and mother. Finally, Beau led Lula to the entrance and everyone stood. The long aisle stretched before him and it seemed as if she would never make it to him. When they finally arrived, she kissed Beau's cheek through the veil and Beau put Lula's hands in Barton's. His heart quaked at the pulse he felt through her fingertips. He'd always thought of her as *his* Lula, but from this moment on, he would also be *her* Barton.

The minister took her wrist and untied the black tie and joined Barton's wrist to hers with it, clasping hands. She'd worn it faithfully since Christmas, he'd never seen her without it, and now, when he wore it, he'd always think of her.

They said their vows and, just as his knees couldn't take another minute of the tension, the minister announced them as husband and wife. Barton turned to his bride and she to him. He found the hem of the veil and lifted it, finally able to see the face of his beautiful wife. She glowed, brilliant before him. Her hand reached for him and he tucked it in his own relishing in the pleasure of holding even just her hands. He pulled her near and kissed her to seal the covenant before their families and before God. And it was good.

Lula's sister Nora ran to the front and hugged them both as he untied the knot of his tie about their wrists so they could walk out of the chapel together. He smiled down at Nora.

Her shy, sweet smile captivated him. He'd never had a sister before, but he did now and he'd protect this precious sister fiercely.

"Barton, I'm supposed to welcome you to the family." She reached up on her toes as she pulled his arm down and kissed him gently on the cheek. "We're so very glad to have you." Her blue eyes, so honest and sweet, lit in a smile. He couldn't help but give her one right back and tugged on one of Nora's loose curls. "Thank you, Butterfly. I don't think I could've found a better family to join."

Lula tucked herself under his arm in the spot where she fit just perfectly, just as he'd thought she would from the first moment she'd walked into his classroom three years before. He tugged on one of her curls, setting it free of one of the pins.

"Barton!" She gasped and reached for it, swatting his hand playfully when he tugged it again. "I can't help it. I won't promise to never tease you."

She smiled, warming him right down to his toes. "Can you at least leave the butter out of it?"

He buried his fingers in her hair and kissed her, loosening every last pin. Today was not a day for regrets, but new beginnings. He pulled away just enough to gently tuck her head under his chin, her hair now spilling loosely over her shoulders. "I don't need butter to get your attention. I promise to love and care for you all the rest of my days."

She held him tightly and he knew, beyond a doubt, that it was true.

Historical Elements

I originally found the city of Spearfish on my honeymoon. My husband and I toured all over the lovely Black Hills and stayed in a cabin near Bridal Veil Falls in Spearfish Canyon. So, when I read about the Spearfish Normal School that not only was a school for teachers, but also had primary students as well... A story was born.

The Spearfish Normal School had many names but began with a government grant in 1883, and continues to educate teachers today. It is now called Black Hills State University.

Despite my best efforts, I was unable to find pictures inside the school, only in front of and around it. Any descriptions inside the building are fictional. Due to a fire in 1925, the buildings I describe in the story are no longer there.

For the purposes of this story, I used rules generally followed by school boards of the late 19th century. Many of those didn't change for a long time. That isn't to say that there weren't progressive schools, there were. But the majority of teachers, especially female teachers, had to live under strict rules. Some as silly as the number of petticoats that had to be worn. Though, I'm not sure who would be in charge of checking on that... Generally speaking, female teachers were not allowed to 'step out', as it were, with any man. They were not allowed to be out later than eight o'clock on a school night, some rule lists even went so far as to say which businesses teachers had to stay away from, heaven forbid they go out for ice cream! While some lists I've seen may have been created or falsified, the fact is, even as late as the 1960s, teachers were held under strict rules of behavior.

Spearfish is a wonderful little town just on the outskirts of the northern Black Hills. It has rich prairies for cattle and farming, but is close to Deadwood and Lead. This provided Spearfish with great revenue opportunities. Spearfish had beef while other areas did not. Spearfish leveraged its lack of gold against the wealth of the prairie and came out the victor, and has stayed relatively prosperous.

For those wondering about the "Roman conqueror" who climbed Bridal Veil Falls, the story is true, but I'm not telling who it was. Thank you, dear reader, for joining me on this adventure. Be sure to join my special reader list to find out when the next Seven Brides of South Dakota novel will be released. You can also get a free book at www.KariTrumbo.com.

Kari Trumbo is an inspirational romance author, blogger and proud home schooling mother to four great kids. She interacts often on reader groups on Facebook and volunteers at the local library when needed. When she isn't writing, she is obsessively reading and expanding her skills as a wordsmith. Kari lives in her great-grandfather's remodeled 1890-built home in central Minnesota with her husband, children, cats, and one hungry wood stove.

Other Titles:

Western Vows

Forsaking All Others
To Honor and Cherish
For Richer or Poorer
To Love and Comfort

Cutter's Creek

Montana Trails
A Lily Blooms
A Penny Shines
A Carol Plays
A Ruby Glows
An Ivy Tangles
Keepsake

Seven Brides of South Dakota

Dreams in Deadwood
Kisses in Keystone
Love in Lead
Romance in Rapid
Sparks in Spearfish
Coming Soon: *Hearts in Hot Springs*

Made in the USA
Middletown, DE
30 May 2018